The Scrapper

**A new departure for the author of the Mrs Browne trilogy:
*The Mammy, The Chisellers, The Granny***

Praise for *The Mammy*

'A born storyteller'
THE LONDON INDEPENDENT

'full of devastating wit'
BOOKS IRELAND

'A story as colourful as Moore Street itself, but there is also
pathos, compassion and irony'
ENTERTAINER

Praise for *The Chisellers*

'it's a brilliant book'
SUNDAY INDEPENDENT

'The characters leap off the page ...
you'll have to buy this book'
SUNDAY WORLD

'full of living and raw humour'
LEINSTER EXPRESS

'great crack'
BOOKS IRELAND

Praise for *The Granny*

'packed with Dublin wit from start to finish'
DERRY PEOPLE

'full of real people, earthy humour and unforgettable characters'
WOMAN'S WAY

An acclaimed author, actor, director, scriptwriter and playwright, Brendan O'Carroll is one of Ireland's most successful entertainers. Over the last fifteen years he has turned his Midas touch on a whole range of projects, from his much-loved radio show, *Mrs Browne's Boys*, to his best-selling novels, *The Mammy*, *The Chisellers* and *The Granny*, his screen debut in Roddy Doyle's *The Van*, his TV quiz show *Hot Milk and Pepper*, his stage successes, the release of the film adaptation of *The Mammy*, (called *Agnes Browne* and starring Anjelica Huston), and the smash-hit success of his TV sitcom, *Mrs Brown's Boys*.

BRENDAN O'CARROLL

The Scrapper

THE O'BRIEN PRESS
DUBLIN

First published as *Sparrow's Trap* 1997 by
The O'Brien Press Ltd.,
12 Terenure Road East, Rathgar, Dublin 6, Ireland.
Tel: +353 1 4923333; Fax: +353 1 4922777
E-mail: books@obrien.ie
Website: www.obrien.ie
This edition published as *The Scrapper*, 2011
Reprinted 2012 (three times), 2013.

ISBN: 978-0-86278-538-3

British Library Cataloguing-in-publication Data
A catalogue record for this title is available from
the British Library

6 7 8 9 10
13 14 15 16

Cover photographs:
Background image by Corrado Bosi.
Image of boy courtesy of Corbis
Typesetting, editing, design, layout:
The O'Brien Press Ltd
Printed and bound by CPI Group (UK) Ltd,
Croydon, CR0 4YY
The paper used in this book is produced using
pulp from managed forests

Dedicated to my two eldest grandsons,
Jamie O'Carroll and Felix Brendan Delany.
Just to say thank you for the joy!

My Father spent his waking hours
inventing dreams to tell
of knights in shining armour
or a witch with an evil spell
but the greatest hero in my life
never slew a dragon dead,
he was just a plain and simple man
that each night tucked me in my bed.

Excerpt from: *Land of Fairytale Dreams*,
by Brendan O'Carroll

INTRODUCTION

Everything has its time and every person will have their day.

This is a lesson I learned from my mother, Maureen O'Carroll. She was an extraordinary woman. Having begun her adult life as a nun, she left a convent when she began to doubt her vocation. She went on to have eleven children, so she was probably right that convent life was not for her. She also became the first woman elected to the Irish Parliament for the Labour Party in 1953 and still all of us lived in a two-bedroomed council house.

The core lesson of all my mother's nuggets of wisdom that she imparted to me is this: ANYTHING is possible, for anyone!

This possibility, I suppose, is also the core of the story of Sparrow McCabe. A man who get his 'shot', but does not understand that sometimes the result of that will not manifest itself for a long time.

I grew up in similar circumstances to Sparrow and in identical surroundings. And you, reader, are witnessing my 'shot'. So far, so good. It is working out for me, but it has taken over twenty-five years for me to see that. On the way I have been blessed with three magnificent children, Fiona, Danny and Eric, and four beautiful grandsons all of whom make every day beautiful for me. I have also met and married a woman, Jennifer Gibney, who saw more in me than I saw in myself. I wish you this good fortune, for truly Jenny has been the decoration on my tree of life that turns it into a glistening Christmas tree.

So then, feet up, get yourself a mug of tea and relax with this book. For believe it or not ... you have just now become a part of my 'shot'.

Brendan O'Carroll
Dublin 2011

PART ONE

CHAPTER ONE

1982
Snuggstown, Dublin

RITA McCABE SAT in her usual corner of the Falcon Inn lounge bar. The celebration was in full swing. She watched her husband Macker move drunkenly from table to table spilling Guinness from his pint on anyone within splashing range. This was his night. She knew it would be only a matter of time before he unzipped his flies and produced his penis to his waiting audience. They would cheer, and she would once again be mortified with embarrassment. It was a ritual with him. It had begun on the evening of 14 September 1957 in this very same pub. Rita hadn't been there that night – she'd been busy delivering her only son. It was that delivery that started Macker's dick-waving ritual.

Macker had accompanied her right to the door of the Rotunda Maternity Hospital. This however was his limit. Beyond that door, the goings-on were 'women's business'. He left the young Rita in the hands of a nurse and her mother as he retired to the Falcon Inn to await a result – to await the result he wanted. A boy. Rita had difficulty in bearing boys, Macker told those in his company. Since their marriage in 1955, miscarriage had followed miscarriage. God knows he had done his bit, but Rita just couldn't seem to carry boys.

Like all the bars in Snuggstown the Falcon Inn was licensed until 11.30pm. But if you were a regular, and Macker was, it was possible to drink on until the early hours of the morning. Macker was just removing the pint glass from his lips when there was a rap at the now-locked door. With a creamy white moustache of Guinness froth over his lip he looked at the bar manager, a childlike fear in his eyes.

'I'll get it,' the manager said flatly as he rose from his stool. There were about thirty other late drinkers in the bar. Every one of them stopped drinking and looked first at Macker, then at the door. The bar was now silent as the deadbolt clacked open.

'Hello, Missus,' was all the manager said as Rita's mother entered. She looked exhausted. She stood just inside the doorway, indicating that she was not staying. Macker looked at her enquiringly. When she spoke her voice was soft.

'It's a boy.'

There was no reaction yet from either Macker or the group. More information was required.

'A healthy boy,' Rita's mother added with a smile.

The place erupted. Macker called for drinks for everyone and regulars queued to shake his hand or slap his back.

'What weight?' called an older man from his stool at the

11

end of the bar. Over the years he had heard many women ask this question. He had no idea why, but it was always a standard question so he asked it anyway.

'Four pounds and six ounces,' the woman called back, and seeing that her task was complete she left. Nobody had congratulated her on the birth of her grandson.

A tall red-haired man approached Macker. 'Four pounds and six ounces? Jesus, that's small.'

Macker was now unsure. 'Is it?' He turned to the bar manager who was busy pulling pints. 'Liam – is it? Is that small?'

'All mine were over the eight-pound mark, sure enough. But he'll be fine – he'll be fine.'

Macker relaxed. Just as he did the red-haired man gripped him in the crotch.

'Well now, Macker. You can't expect to catch a shark with a worm!'

There was a roar of laughter from the crowd, and Macker joined in. However, unwilling to let this slight on his manhood pass he stood on the bar counter, unzipped his fly and produced his penis, to roars of approval.

'There's not a shark off the coast of Ireland that wouldn't mind *this* for his dinner!' Macker roared, as he fell backwards into the arms of his laughing friends.

As Macker and his friends drank into the early hours, a few miles away the four-pound six-ounce boy, later to be christened Anthony Jude, slept peacefully, recuperating from the first of many battles he would face as Snuggstown's newest arrival.

★ ★ ★

And so here they were, twenty-five years after Sparrow's birth. Same pub. Same scenario. Rita tried to recall all the events since her son's birth that had heralded the flashing of her husband's 'love truncheon', as he liked to call it. She sipped on her Pimms No 1. Seven – no, eight! Sparrow's christening, Sparrow's confirmation, Sparrow's first boxing title win – that was the schools' championship. His three national title wins, and his selection for the Irish Olympic boxing team. The latter was somewhat premature, as Sparrow was later de-selected because of a hand injury. Macker was disappointed, she remembered, and God love him he didn't know what to do with his mickey then. He didn't have a ritual for disappointment.

'Speech!' someone called from the crowd to Macker. As usual Macker feigned reluctance, but then put his drink down and raised a hand for silence. He got it. After wiping his chin he began.

'I can't tell yeh all how proud I am of me son, Sparrow.'

'Sure the whole of Snuggstown is proud of him, Macker!' someone interjected, and a roar of approval went up.

Again Macker held his hand aloft. Once again the silence came.

'Eh, thank you, Tommy, and indeed all of you. Sparrow's win tonight was decisive and nobody can now deny that his shot at the European title is legitimate. Menendez can't avoid my boy now.'

'The cowardly Spanish bastard!' Another interjection, met this time with groans of discontent rather than a cheer.

13

'That may be,' Macker continued, 'but he's a good fuckin' scrapper!'

The room now went quiet.

Macker smiled, 'But not good enough for my little Sparrow.'

Now a huge cheer filled the lounge bar. At last came the loaded question.

'And where did the Sparrow come from, Macker?'

There followed a spontaneous burst of song: 'Macker, Macker, show us your flute, show us your flute, show us your flute. Macker, Macker ...'

Rita closed her eyes. She fixed a pretend smile on her face to hide her disgust as her husband danced in the background with his penis dangling like a demented raw sausage. With her eyes closed she drifted into a dream of yet another scenario for her husband's death. She was jarred from her thoughts by a nudge.

'Move over in the bed, Rita.' It was Dolly Coffey. Rita moved up a little on the bench seat and Dolly plonked herself into a space about half the width of her arse.

'Yeh must be very proud, love. A shot at the European Championship!'

Rita took another sip of her Pimms. 'Oh I am, Dolly, I am proud. I just wish it was something other than boxing. I hate it! So many nights in the last ten years Anthony has come home battered, bruised, with every joint in his body swollen; it's not a good sport for mothers.'

'No, I suppose it's not.'

The two were quiet for a while, taking in the celebration. Now and then Dolly would shoot a sideways glance at Rita. If anyone were watching the two women, and no one was, it would have been obvious to them that Dolly had something on her mind. When Dolly spoke again her words were very deliberate.

'Sparrow's down in my house with our Eileen.' Again the sideways glance at Rita, and Dolly continued, 'A right pair of fuckin' love-birds, what?'

The two women laughed. Dolly was waiting on a reply, and it came. 'She's a good strong girl, Dolly. You done a fine job with her,' Rita complimented.

'Thanks, Rita, you can only do your best when there's nine to be rarin'.' Dolly accepted the compliment gracefully.

Like synchronised swimmers both women took a sip of their drinks.

'You have one for confirmation in March, haven't yeh?' Rita was now enjoying the chat and lit up a cigarette, indicating that she was getting settled. Dolly, with a mouthful of Guinness, nodded before she answered.

'Yeh, young Paul – the little bastard! I don't know what I'm going to do with him. He's out robbin' cars at night, no sense of responsibility. I've warned him – I'm tellin' his father and he'll put manners on him. I don't know where he gets it!' Dolly sounded exasperated.

'His father will straighten him out, Dolly, when he's out.' Rita took a drag of her cigarette and then continued. 'When is he home?'

'Well, he got nine but he'll only serve three. Should be out by the end of the month,' Dolly replied, still genuinely not knowing where young Paul had got it from.

'That's nice.' Rita took another drink. 'God – confirmation, there's a day out in the church for yeh, Dolly.'

Dolly now saw her chance. She looked Rita straight in

the eyes and her reply was measured.

'Rita ... I think we could be in the church before that!' She held Rita's gaze.

Rita froze, her cigarette halfway to her lips. 'What do you mean, Dolly?' she asked.

CHAPTER TWO

ANTHONY 'SPARROW' McCABE had a lump the size of a golf ball over his right eye. His left eyelid was swollen and looked particularly sore where the four stitches were. His top lip was puffed up beneath the dark brown moustache, and his cheekbones were every colour of the rainbow. Even so, it was obvious, thanks to the sparkling blue eyes and impish smile, that when the swelling and discolouration were gone, Eileen Coffey had the cutest-looking boyfriend in Snuggstown. It was not just because of his small frame that Anthony had earned the nickname Sparrow, but because of the animated way he moved when he spoke, like a tiny sparrow flitting from tree to tree. He was excited now, and looked more sparrow-like than ever, his words spilling from his mouth.

'Please marry me, Eileen,' Sparrow pleaded.

'I will. Yeh know I will, Sparrow McCabe, but not yet. I will after the baby is born.' She tried to calm him.

Sparrow glowed at the thought of his new baby. He smiled at Eileen as best he could, and laid his hand gently on her stomach. Her pregnancy wasn't obvious, but he was sure he could feel a tiny heartbeat. With small movements he began to rub her tummy. She looked down at his hand. His knuckles were swollen and purple, yet his touch was as light as an angel's feather. He snuggled into her neck.

'Next year when I'm European champion, Eileen, will yeh marry me then?'

'I don't care if you're world champion as long as you're you. My sparrow.' Eileen put her arms gently around him. They lay there on the couch, in their own little world bordered by each other's arms. Sparrow placed his other hand on Eileen's knee and slowly began to move it along her thigh. He moved it sideways until he could now feel both thighs, one with his palm, one with the back of his hand. Gently Eileen pushed her thighs together, hugging Sparrow's probing hand. Then the door burst open. In the door-frame stood both mothers, Dolly and Rita. It was Sparrow's mother, Rita, who spoke:

'Right then, lover boy. Let's talk about this weddin'.'

* * *

As they came out of St Catherine's church the bride and groom were aglow with joy. The wedding attire made the couple look rich and feel important, even if their size made them look as though they had just stepped off the top of the wedding cake. Eileen was startled by the amount of camera flashes, she hadn't realised the extent of the press interest – and they *were* interested. For just two days before the wedding Lorenzo Menendez had finally announced that he would fight Sparrow for the European lightweight title. This had already prompted headlines such as: 'New groom will sweep clean' or 'Hitch the maiden, ditch the Spaniard'.

The wedding reception that followed was full of joy and laughter. Macker delivered a wonderful speech on behalf of the groom's family, and was under strict orders that at no stage during the evening was his penis to be produced.

'What are you goin' to do?' Macker had asked Rita that morning. 'Stitch me fly up?'

'No,' Rita replied and produced a shiny stainless-steel kitchen knife. 'But let me tell yeh this, if you take out your willie I'll be takin' out this,' she waved the knife menacingly. 'And then,' she added, 'your dreams will come true, your willie *will* touch the floor.'

Later that evening at the reception, when Rita and Dolly had a couple of drinks under their belts, Rita told Dolly the story of the confrontation that morning and both women howled with laughter. It was clear to everybody that whatever way the marriage went the mothers-in-law were going to be firm friends.

CHAPTER THREE

SIXTY-FOUR MILES AWAY on the same night that Sparrow and Eileen were celebrating their marriage, another ceremony was taking place. The venue was somewhat different; it was Templemore police training centre. Seventy-four graduates, their families, girlfriends, and in some cases wives, were partying and celebrating the culmination of three years' hard training. The young men looked quite dashing in their full dress uniforms. Although drink was flowing freely, they were careful to be on their best behaviour because as usual the function was attended by the 'brass' of the police force. One young graduate, Kieran Clancy, stood leaning against a pillar watching the dancing and taking in the joy of the celebration. One hundred young men had joined this class three years ago and only seventy-four had made it through to the finish. Kieran had been placed top of the class.

'Christ, I'm after losin' a whore of a button!'

Kieran turned towards Michael Malone, the owner of the deep west-of-Ireland voice. The Galway man, with the close-cropped ginger hair, was in a flap.

'You what?' Kieran asked calmly.

'I'm after losin' a bloody button.' Malone repeated his statement, sounding as if he had lost the crown jewels.

Kieran smiled, casually glanced around the room, then fixed his eyes on a spot and pointed. 'There it is, there, look, just under that table.'

The other man beamed a smile. 'Ah sweet Jaysus, Kieran, you're amazing. Thanks a lot,' and he rushed off to get the button.

Kieran Clancy's mother had told him from a very early age that he had St Anthony's gift, the gift of finding things. If anything were lost in their home in Dublin, Kieran's mother would simply say, 'Just wait till Kieran comes in from school and he'll find it.' And he usually did, although he regarded it as a 'knack' rather than a gift.

Confirmation of this knack of his came when he was about thirteen years of age, on a day out at the beach with his mother and father and some relations. Some of Kieran's aunts and uncles were swimming while he was sitting on a towel on the sand with his mother, devouring sandwiches. Kieran's Aunt Maeve returned from the water dripping wet and looking so cold that even her goose bumps had goose bumps. She was about to take a sandwich when she suddenly exclaimed, 'Good Lord, my ring! I've lost my wedding ring!'

Kieran's mother got Maeve to take Kieran and herself out to where she had been swimming. 'It was about here,' she told them, 'but you can't even see in the water it's so clouded with sand.'

'Don't worry,' Kieran's mother said, and she simply nodded at Kieran. Kieran was now standing up to his thighs in seawater. He bent over and dug his hands deep into the sand beneath the water; slowly he brought them up and, as the water washed the sand from his hands, there on his little finger was a gold wedding band.

'I don't believe it!' shrieked Maeve. 'You're a marvel! Betty, that child definitely has St Anthony's gift.'

When at eighteen years of age Kieran had announced to his mother that he wished to become a member of the Garda Síochána she showed little surprise, and her only comment was, 'Well, with St Anthony's gift you'll probably make a great detective.' Detective Kieran Clancy: he liked the sound of that.

Now Kieran stood there on his graduation night, a tiny smile on his face as those memories came floating back to him. He didn't know he was being watched.

***

Moya Connolly had not planned to come to the graduation this evening. She had been on the verge of a tantrum, insisting she wasn't attending yet another graduation ball with her father, the Police Commissioner. She was a beautiful girl and her father loved to show her off – with her red hair, pale skin and green eyes she looked the typical Irish colleen. But an Irish colleen without a boyfriend. For with fiery red hair came a fiery temper, and although many's the man and boy had tried, none could tie her down. Exasperated, her father often said, 'No man will pick Moya, 'tis Moya will pick her own man.'

Unknown to her father, that very night Moya was making her choice. She looked Kieran Clancy over again and again: his blond hair, the high cheek bones and the strong chin. That mischievous glint in his eye.

Moya's mother sat down beside her at the circular table, which still had the remains of the evening's dinner scattered around it. 'His name is Clancy, Kieran Clancy,' she announced. 'He comes from Rathfarnham. He's twenty-three years of age and he wants to be a detective.'

Moya was stunned at first, then burst out laughing. 'Oh Mum, you're a tonic – you should have been in Intelligence.'

'I often think I am, dear, and have been all my life.'

The two women laughed, then Moya became a little more serious. 'He is nice, isn't he, Mum?'

'Gorgeous. And he graduated top of the class, just like your father.' Both women were now looking at Kieran.

'Oh Mum, I swore I'd never fall for a policeman.'

'So did I, love.' Again the two women laughed.

As they watched Kieran, Moya's father approached him and began to speak to him.

'What's Dad doing?' Moya wondered aloud.

'He's going to introduce him to us – I asked him to.'

'Oh Mum, for heaven's sake!'

They saw the two men chat, Kieran now out of his casual pose and standing erect, military-style. After a few moments the Commissioner raised his hand, indicated their table, and the two began to make their way towards Moya and her mother.

'Good God, he's bringing him over.'

'Well, of course he is! What did you expect him to do – shout the introduction across the room? Just be calm, dear, for goodness sake.'

Moya tried to be as casual as possible when the two men eventually reached the table. Kieran Clancy was even more attractive close up than he had been from a distance. He shook the Commissioner's wife's hand very formally and then turned to Moya. He took her hand in his, and was in the middle of saying 'How do you do' when his expression changed completely. Carmel Connolly looked at her husband and smiled. The Commissioner smiled back. They were both recalling a similar situation thirty years previously – and, surprisingly, the Commissioner blushed.

CHAPTER FOUR

BY ANY STANDARDS, it was a beautiful house. Sheila Murtagh had convinced her husband Dennis to allow her to do all five bedrooms in different colours, although Dennis himself would have gone for plain white throughout, reflecting his keep-it-simple attitude, an attitude every bank manager needed. The Murtaghs had three children and three children's bedrooms, although only two of them were being used, as the two boys shared bunk-beds in one of the rooms. They were sound asleep right now. In the other occupied bedroom was Deirdre, the Murtagh's eldest child and only daughter. She was sixteen and had all the trappings of a sixteen-year-old's lifestyle scattered around her room. Deirdre was in her room, but she wasn't asleep. She would have found it very difficult to sleep in the position she was in, spread-eagled on the bed, face up, with an arm tied to each of the top bed posts and a leg tied to each of the bottom bed posts. Her eyes were tightly closed and across her mouth was a strip of surgical tape. She was breathing heavily through her nose and through the tape one could just hear her murmur, 'Hail Mary, full of grace ...'

Downstairs in one of the two carver chairs in the dining room sat Sheila Murtagh. Her legs were tied to the legs of the chair and her arms to the beautiful hand-carved arm rests. She too had surgical tape across her mouth, but unlike her daughter who was unscathed, Sheila had bruises and small cuts across her forehead and down the left side of her face. She seemed to be sleeping soundly, but actually she had passed out some fifteen minutes earlier from overwhelming fear.

Half-way down the hall, and through two french doors, was the main living room. On the pink velour couch and its matching armchairs sat three men, smoking and talking.

The two that sat on the couch were easily identifiable as brothers; they were Bubbles and Teddy Morgan. The Morgans were large men and had been inseparable since their early childhood. They had been in school together, they had been in borstal together, they went to parties together, and they had been in prison together. The two were a bit of an enigma, you see, for Bubbles had no capacity to think, so Teddy had to think for both of them, and Teddy had difficulty even in thinking for himself! Neither was married, nor had either a girlfriend, although Teddy had been in love for a short time with a girl called Eileen Coffey. Though this love was never reciprocated, Teddy always regarded Eileen as 'his girl'. Unfortunately for Teddy, Eileen was getting married that day, which probably accounted for his grumpy humour, the brunt of which had been taken by Sheila Murtagh in the kitchen. Neither of the two men was speaking; instead they were completely focused on and listening to the third man in the room.

This was Simon Williams. In Snuggstown he was known as Simple Simon, not because Simon was retarded in any way – quite the opposite. Simon was a very intelligent, very sharp man. He'd got his nickname 'Simple' because that was the first word Simon used to solve any problem. If somebody ruffled Simon's feathers, Simon's answer would be, 'Simple, break his legs.'

'Some day I'm going to have a house like this boy's.' Simon spoke softly as he glanced around the room. 'Yeh see, lads, it's all about application. It's not enough to think you want to do something, you have to go and do it. And people have to know that you're that kind of man. They have to know that if you say you're going to do something you will, without fail. That's how you get respect, lads. You take the arse-hole who owns this house. If I walked into his office yesterday and talked to him about, let's say, starting a new business, do you think he'd give me respect? I don't think so. But two seconds after he walks through that door you watch the kind of respect we get.'

'And will yeh still live in Snuggstown, Mr Williams?' Although the conversation had moved on, Bubbles Morgan was still at the house stage.

'You must be joking, Bubbles! I don't want to *live* in Snuggstown, I just want to *own* it, and then I'll live somewhere else.'

'You will, Mr Williams, you will own it!' Teddy knew the right things to say. Simon smiled slightly; he enjoyed adoration, albeit from fools. The beam of two headlights swung across the room as a car pulled into the driveway of the Murtagh home.

'Aye, aye lads, here's our man.'

'Let's hope he has the keys, Mr Williams,' Teddy commented.

'Oh he has the keys all right, if not he'll find them – otherwise we'll bash the door of the bank down with his daughter's head.'

The other two men began to laugh and Simon had to shush them with a finger over his lips.

Dennis Murtagh climbed out of the car, slammed the door and went around to the boot from where he extracted his golf clubs. He used the brass Yale key to open the garage door, and he left the clubs just inside. It had been a tough game, he hadn't played well and he was tired. He hoped to go straight to bed, and in the back of his mind prayed that his wife was not in the humour for a chat. As he walked across the driveway to the front door the exterior light was switched on by a motion sensor. He let himself into the outer hall, closed the door and double-locked it, then went through the french doors into the hallway itself. He stood for a moment with his mouth agape. Three bulky figures stood before him, their faces covered by stocking masks. One thing he noticed that would stick with him for the rest of his life was that the middle figure had a Trilby hat on over the stocking mask. The other two held pistols. In unison the three cried, 'Surprise!'

CHAPTER FIVE

SPARROW AND EILEEN HAD A SHORT HONEYMOON of ten days in Galway city. Although Eileen still had fourteen weeks to go before the birth of the baby the couple did nothing over-energetic; instead they spent their days taking short walks, eating and talking. In the evenings they would have a couple of drinks and then eagerly look forward to going to bed together, not just for lovemaking but for the pleasure of being there with each other. Neither Sparrow nor Eileen had ever, as adults, experienced that feeling of falling into a deep sleep with somebody else's arm around you, and then waking up every morning to have beside you the one person you wanted in life. It was a great honeymoon. But when they returned to Dublin at the end of the ten days the honeymoon was well and truly over. Tommy Molloy, Sparrow's coach, saw to that.

Tommy had chosen The Star And Crescent Boxing Club as Sparrow's training camp for the next two months. Although it was only thirty miles from Dublin, in Drogheda, Tommy had arranged digs there for the entire team, and for two months Sparrow would not see Eileen. They talked every morning and every night on the telephone, but as the training went on these conversations became shorter and shorter and Eileen could tell that Sparrow was getting more and more focused on his fight. Tommy Molloy had arranged flights and accommodation for Macker, Rita and Eileen out to Madrid. But Sparrow would be travelling ten days beforehand for acclimatisation, training, and, of course, to meet the press. By the time the night of the fight arrived and Eileen, along with Macker and Rita, stepped from the cab into the entrance of the stadium, Eileen had not seen her husband for twelve weeks. And Sparrow had only seen the progress of her pregnancy in photographs sent to him by his mother. These are the sacrifices that have to be made for a thirty-minute grasp at glory.

In the dressing room Tommy Molloy taped Sparrow's hands tightly, all the while speaking to him: 'You are the champ. You will be the champ. This guy is no match for you. You want it more than he wants it.' This last phrase sent Sparrow into a reverie. Sparrow had long ago realised that he was never going to be academically bright. His only route out of Snuggstown to fame and fortune and a secure future for his wife and child would come either through music or sport. Sparrow couldn't sing or play an instrument, but he could box. This was his shot, his ticket out. In the ten days since he had arrived in Madrid he had read articles about Lorenzo Menendez. He could have been reading about himself – similar background, similar amateur fighting success. Similar. Similar. The winner would move on, probably to a world title chance, the loser would go back to Snuggstown, or Santa de la Snuggstown or whatever. Tommy Molloy slapped Sparrow hard across the face. Sparrow snapped out of his reverie with anger.

'That's it, Sparrow, you want it more than he does,' Molloy was screaming at him now.

As is traditional, everybody left the dressing room two minutes before the fight. Sparrow sat alone. Then slowly he stood up and walked to the end of the room to the full-length mirror. He was afraid, very afraid – not afraid of being hurt, he'd been hurt before, and wounds heal. He didn't know what he was afraid of, but there was something, something ... He looked at his body from top to bottom: he had never looked better, he had never felt better. He was ready. He spoke to his reflection.

'I want it more than he does.' He said it again and again, the last time screaming at himself. 'I want it more than he does!!' The dressing-room door opened. Tommy Molloy stuck his head in and announced, 'It's time, Sparrow.'

The Sanmartino stadium in Madrid was hot and heaving with bodies. As Macker, Rita and Eileen were led to their ringside seats the noise of the crowd was deafening. The two women sat quietly. Macker remained standing. Slowly Macker turned full circle to take in the huge crowd that seemed to sweep away from the ringside straight up to the roof of the massive building on all sides. Here and there he could see Irish flags, but the red and yellow of Spain was everywhere, and the crowd chanted 'Men-en-dez' in unison over and over again. Macker defiantly puffed out his chest and smiled as he slowly sat down. At the ringside the Irish radio commentator Jimmy Magee spotted Sparrow's family. He waved and they acknowledged his wave, then he returned to his microphone to tell the folks listening back home that the family had arrived.

The MC stepped through the ropes and took his position in the centre of the ring. In his left hand he held some papers. He was dressed in a dinner suit and bow tie, with his hair slicked back. He looked like a head waiter about to read the contents of a menu rather than a man about to introduce two 'pitbulls' into the ring for a slaughter. Slowly, from above the MC, a microphone dropped out of the lights. When it reached his shoulder the MC took it in his right hand.

'Ladies and Gentlemen, Sanmartino Stadium, in association with De La Cruz Fruits, are proud to present the sixth bout on your card this evening. The bout is to decide the European Lightweight Championship Title. Let me first introduce the challenger. Wearing white trunks and weighing one hundred and twenty-four pounds, from Ireland, Anthony "The Sparrow" McCabe.'

A spotlight came on from the back of the stadium, focusing on the dressing-room doors and directing everyone's attention to them. The crowd stood up. Rita McCabe's heart shuddered as she beheld the tiny figure of her only child, dressed for battle.

Macker screamed, 'Yea, Sparrow!' His scream was primeval and animal-like. It frightened Rita even more than she was already frightened. Rita looked at Eileen. Sparrow's new wife did not stand or clap, but sat looking down at her knees. As Sparrow began to make his way to the ring the crowd booed and cat-called at this young man whom they had never met and had only barely seen before. Rita placed her hand on Macker's arm. 'They hate him,' she said.

'Of course they do, woman, they're Spanish! What did you expect, for fuck's sake?' Macker roared back as he roughly shrugged away her hand.

'Kill the bastard, Sparrow!' he yelled as Sparrow stepped into the ring. This scream was even wilder than before. There was spit dribbling down his chin and his eyes were bulging.

Staring at her husband, Rita slowly sat down. She was sorry she'd come; she should have stayed at home and listened to it on the radio as usual. She felt Eileen's hand on hers, and it was cold. She took it. The women's fingers interlocked and their terrified eyes met.

If the derisory booing had unsettled Sparrow, he didn't show it. As Tommy Molloy massaged his neck and shoulders, Sparrow had a perfectly calm look about him. His eyes were glazed as if he was in a trance. Every square inch of his body was ready for this fight. Were an artist to be given clay and asked to mould it into a Grecian Olympian model, the result would have resembled the tiny Irishman in the white trunks. His body was ready. All that mattered now was his mind. As he finished his massage, Tommy Molloy took Sparrow's head firmly in his hands. He brought his face up to Sparrow's until their noses touched. He locked eyes with Sparrow and spoke strongly but calmly, 'You want it more than he does.'

Sparrow nodded.

'If you weaken he'll kill you.'

Sparrow nodded again.

Then, with a smile, Tommy said, 'I love you.'

Sparrow hadn't been expecting that! Nervously he began to laugh and Tommy joined in, their laughter drowned in the boom of the MC's voice.

'And now, Ladies and Gentleman, the defending champion.'

The crowd exploded into a deafening roar that really scared Rita and Eileen. It went on and on, so loud that the stadium actually shook, and so long that all that was heard from the MC was the final '... Lorenzo "The Village Boy" Menendez.' And the roar took off again as the olive-skinned man appeared in the spotlight.

Lorenzo Menendez looked super-fit. His close-cropped, jet-black hair was shining, his skin was sleek and oiled, and as he walked down the aisle his long red satin trunks shimmered in such a way that they looked like a flame about his thighs. He moved like a ballet dancer. He looked class, and although just one pound heavier than Sparrow, to Sparrow's mother he seemed to be twice the size of her son. Eileen didn't even look.

* * *

'Is this him?' Bubbles Morgan asked his older brother.

'No.' Teddy replied without seeming to open his eyes. The two men were sitting in Simon Williams's Ford Granada outside of the Fionn McCool pub. The public house had been closed for a couple of months while it was being renovated following a fire. Their boss Simon Williams was inside attending the official re-opening party. Simon had instructed his two henchmen to wait outside in the car. The last time the Morgan brothers had been in the pub was before the fire. In fact it was just seconds before the fire, which had broken out at 3am in mysterious circumstances. Tonight Simon was attending the opening by personal invitation of the owner, who coincidentally had now taken out anti-fire insurance with Simon for a modest weekly sum. Bubbles was bored.

'D'yeh know what, Teddy?' he asked.

'What?'

'If a train was travelling at a hundred miles an hour and a fly was coming the other way and they met head-on, the train would stop!'

Teddy slowly opened one eye and looked at his brother suspiciously.

Bubbles detected the doubt in his brother's myopic gaze. 'If the fly was going a hundred miles an hour too,' Bubbles added as if to qualify his amazing statement.

Teddy now opened both eyes and sat up a little. 'A fuckin' fly can't go a hundred miles an hour!' There was a moment of silence before Teddy lay back again and closed his eyes.

'He could if he was on a train,' Bubbles said quietly.

'Shut the fuck up, Bubbles, will yeh,' Teddy grunted. Again, for a few moments, there was silence.

'Teddy?' Bubbles asked quietly.

'Now what?' Teddy snapped.

'Can I turn on the radio?'

'Yeh. Just so long as ye shut up!'

'Okay.' Bubbles switched on the car radio and Jimmy Magee's voice blasted into the car, live from the Sanmartino Stadium in Madrid. Behind his voice the crowd was manic.

The Spaniard moves forward again, two quick left jabs, both have got through. McCabe counters with a jab and right-hand drive. He didn't catch Menendez properly, but it hurt. The Village Boy felt that one ...'

'Hey Teddy, it's Sparrow's fight!' Bubbles enthused.

Teddy did not move, but his eyes opened.

'*Menendez backs away, Sparrow goes after him. Oh! A three-punch combination from the Irish champion – one to the body, two to the head, lightning fast, and Menendez didn't know where they came from. What a gutsy performance from the young man from Snuggstown. He's not at all overawed by the champion.*'

'Go on, Sparrow!' Bubbles cheered.

'Shut up,' Teddy snarled.

'But he's one of our own, Teddy,' Bubbles countered.

'Shut the fuck up!' Teddy snapped again.

Just then the rear door of the car opened and Simon Williams climbed in. Teddy quickly turned off the radio, and started the engine.

'What are you two shouting about?' Simon asked.

The two brothers looked at each other. 'We were just listening to the fight, Mr Williams,' Bubbles said.

Simon lit a cigar. 'Oh yeh!' he smiled. 'Sparrow McCabe is fighting tonight, isn't he? Turn it back on!'

Bubbles wore a big smile as he twisted the knob of the radio while looking at Teddy. Teddy scowled at him.

'*And from where I sit I can see Sparrow's young wife, Eileen. She has her hands over her face, and well she might as the Spaniard had his best period in the fight so far. A big right hand from Menendez, and the Sparrow rocks again.*'

Simon leaned forward and spoke to Teddy. 'Eileen? Isn't that your old flame, Teddy?'

Teddy didn't reply. He fixed his gaze on the road ahead. Simon sat back. Teddy glanced in the rear-view mirror, and he could see the thin smile on Simon's face. Barely audible and with hardly a movement of his lips Teddy mumbled, 'Come on, Menendez.'

***

Kieran Clancy tripped lightly down the steps of the Connolly home. He was doing his impersonation of Gene Kelly. When he came to the bottom he leaped over the gate and spread his arms wide as he did a spin. Moya was standing on the porch watching him. She clapped gleefully and laughed.

'Go home, you fool,' she chided.

'I'm a fool, all right, a fool for love!' Kieran sang back.

From an upstairs window the deep voice of Moya's father growled. 'Quiet, down there.'

The two laughed. Then Kieran blew a silent kiss to Moya. She waved him away and went into the house giggling.

Kieran was a happy man. Just a couple of months a member of the Gardaí and already he was looking at an appointment to a Dublin station. He was currently stationed in Cootehill in County Cavan. He had a long drive ahead of him tonight. He had made the drive down to Dublin that evening; one hundred miles down and one hundred miles back, all to see Moya for just one hour. It was worth it. He climbed into his Ford Escort and as he turned the ignition the radio came on automatically.

'*Des Kelly Carpets – we buy by the mile, so you save by the yard!*' Then came a short burst of music identifying the sports programme, and Jimmy Magee's voice crackled across the air.

'*Welcome back to Madrid. Well, what a humdinger this fight has turned out to be. The first two rounds were fairly even; if anything they could be shaded in favour of Sparrow McCabe. Then Champion Menendez went to town. He pulled out all the stops;*

37

rounds three, four, and five all ending decisively in his favour.
McCabe had taken a bucketful of punishment. But he was still there
and came out of the sixth more determined than ever. He brought the
fight to the champ and although McCabe has suffered a cut to the
right eye, that I suspect came from a clash of heads, he has taken both
the sixth and seventh rounds. We have three rounds to go and by my
reckoning the scores are all even, but it's McCabe who seems to be
getting on top. From here I can see trainer Tommy Molloy and
McCabe's cut-man Johnny Brough working furiously on that cut
now; if they can keep it closed the Irish boy could just about take this
title, and he would certainly deserve it. There's the bell for the eighth
round.'

Kieran had by now pulled onto the Navan road and was
heading north. He settled back with a smile of admiration on
his face to listen to the rest of the fight.

'Fair play to you, Sparrow,' he said aloud and slapped
his thigh.

*** *** ***

The bell clanged loudly for the eighth round. Sparrow could
hear it, but it seemed to be miles away, not just in another
place but in another dimension.

'He's on the run! Go after him!' Molloy's voice boomed
at Sparrow. Sparrow felt the pressure of his cut-man's thumb
coming off his eye.

'Keep it covered, for fuck's sake – don't let him open it
anymore,' Johnny Brough roared.

The perspiration was stinging Sparrow's eyes. He stood
up, and felt the stool rub across the backs of his legs as it was

whipped away from beneath him. Molloy rammed the gumshield into Sparrow's mouth. It was in crooked. Sparrow straightened it with his tongue. With three paces Sparrow was in the centre of the ring. He was alone. Menendez had not arrived yet. Sparrow knew it then. He knew Menendez had lost his thirst for the fight. It's all over, he thought. I have him.

'Keep it covered,' came the scream from his corner. 'Keep the fuckin' thing covered,' they shouted again.

What? Sparrow thought. Oh yeh, the eye.

Menendez came into focus. He had both gloves in front of his face, and all that was visible to Sparrow was a little triangle, an eye in each corner and the bridge of a nose at the bottom. Menendez's body was exposed.

Sparrow let fly a right. Menendez's eyes bulged at the impact just below his ribcage. A burst of air left his lungs, carrying blood-soaked spittle with it as it gushed from the Spaniard's mouth. Sparrow was sprayed with blood.

Sparrow's mind was on automatic now: throw a second body-punch – quick – before he has a chance to breathe – when the lungs are deflated, that's when the ribs are at their most vulnerable.

The punch left Sparrow's shoulder even before the thought was complete. Thud! Followed by a crack. One of the Spaniard's ribs had gone; Sparrow's eyes widened with the recognition of the sound of bone shattering. The training, the practice, the pain, the sweat, it was all coming to fruition. Sparrow's instinct knew what to do. He dropped his shoulder to feign a third body-punch. If the text books were right the Spaniard should drop his arms to cover the injured rib. The text books were right. As if in slow motion Sparrow saw the gloves of the Spaniard drop from his face. He was wide open. The Spaniard realised his mistake when his gloves had reached his chest. Too late. The momentum allowed the Spaniard's gloves to sink another three inches before he began to bring them back up. Too late. Sparrow was focused on his spot.

'Catch him clean!' he heard Molloy scream from the corner as he threw his body behind the upper-cut. Right on the button. The speed and power from the punch threw the Spaniard's head back far enough to cut off the blood supply momentarily from the spine to the brain. His legs began to buckle. Menendez staggered back against the ropes. The crowd screamed in anguish. Above the din Macker screamed, 'Kill him! Go for it, kill him!'

Sparrow advanced quickly on Menendez. To prevent himself from falling through the ropes Menendez spread his arms wide. It was all over. Sparrow placed his left leg forward to give himself perfect leverage for the final punch. As his foot planted itself squarely on the canvas Sparrow drew back his right arm. The Spaniard knew what was coming. He could do nothing but wait for that millisecond it would take for Sparrow's punch to arrive. He felt so, so tired. The pain of his shattered ribs was so fierce that he couldn't breathe. In a way, the punch would be welcome.

***

Simple Simon leaned forward, excitement in his face. He tried to get closer to the radio; he felt as if he was in the ring with Sparrow.

'Go for it, Sparrow,' Bubbles cried.

'Kill him, kill him!' Simon growled.

***

Kieran Clancy had passed through Navan and was heading for Kells. He was slapping the dashboard of the Ford Escort.

'Go for it! Go on, Sparrow! Take your chance now!' His radio boomed out the commentary.

'What a beautiful upper-cut! The Spaniard staggers away. He's going down – no! Saved by the ropes. McCabe moves forward, he winds up for the big one ...'

***

Simple Simon was banging the back of Teddy's seat. He was jumping up and down like a little child. 'Nail him! Nail him!'

***

Kieran Clancy's car wobbled slightly on the road as he banged the steering wheel. 'Yes, Sparrow! Throw the punch, throw the punch!'

***

Menendez looked up into Sparrow's face; he wished to be eyeball-to-eyeball with his opponent as he went out. He expected to see that look he had seen before, the savage, lustful animal look of the beast as it finishes off the prey. But that's not what he saw. He saw tears, he saw doubt – the

41

punch was not coming.

Sparrow watched as Menendez stumbled away after the upper-cut. It was clumsy. It reminded Sparrow of the way a beautiful bird falls, when it is shot from the skies. As soon as the bullet pierced its downy body it ceased to be a bird. For a bird has grace. Style. It has dynamic in its movement. So this thing that falls, tumbling, ugly, from the air is no longer a bird. Instinctively Sparrow followed his target. Automatically he positioned himself perfectly. Of its own accord his right arm wound up for the final punch. He focused on Menendez's face. It was battered, bloody and bruised. It was ugly. This is no longer a fighter, Sparrow thought. The man was beaten. Victory was one thing, but humiliation another. For a moment the Spaniard's face changed to Sparrow's own face.

Sparrow sprang back.

'Jesus Christ!! What are you doing? Finish him off!' came the scream from his corner. Even the referee now looked at Sparrow, puzzled. Concerned that Sparrow had seen something in the Spaniard's face that he had not, the referee tried to move closer to check.

Tommy Molloy was slamming the canvas with his hands, screaming. 'What in God's name are you doing, Sparrow? Throw the fuckin' punch!'

Sparrow turned to Tommy and indicated with a wave of his gloves that everything was all right, he knew he had done enough. This was his second mistake. The referee felt himself being pushed aside as Menendez lunged passed him. Sparrow's hands were down by his sides and he was mouthing something to his corner. The Spaniard let fly.

Three hours later Sparrow sat ashen-faced in the

waiting room of St Bernadette's hospital just a mile from the stadium, the anguish of defeat completely overshadowed by Eileen's delivery of their stillborn daughter. Rita McCabe was right: boxing is not a sport for mothers.

PART TWO

(1996 – fourteen years later)

CHAPTER SIX

Tuesday, 3 December 1996

IN THE KILMOON HOUSE HOTEL one hundred and sixty people were gathered, all either members or guests of the Kilmoon Chamber of Commerce. They had come together to be addressed by Bernard McCarthy. A member of the Dáil, the Irish Parliament, for twenty-five years, McCarthy was now a Junior Minister with the dubious portfolio of Industrial Incentive. Nobody in the general public knew exactly what Industrial Incentive meant or indeed what this Junior Minister should be doing, and this seemed to suit Bernard McCarthy fine. At every Chamber of Commerce annual lunch it was customary to have a guest speaker – the status of your speaker usually reflected the status of your Chamber of Commerce. The attendance today of a Junior Minister put the Kilmoon Junior Chamber of Commerce in the top twenty percent, so regardless of what Bernard McCarthy said the members would be happy enough. This was just as well, for Bernard McCarthy, after many years in politics, had perfected a talent for spending thirty-five minutes saying absolutely nothing. He would punctuate his speech with remarks like, 'And I pledge to you', or one of his favourites, 'My integrity is well known within this constituency.'

In the carpark of the hotel just at the back of the function room the Minister's limousine waited, along with its chauffeur. Just outside the door of the function room itself stood the Minister's two police bodyguards.

Kieran Clancy's eyebrows shot up as he heard Bernard McCarthy use a new phrase: 'I cannot stress enough how highly I regard the work of the Chambers of Commerce in this country; they are the driving force of the machinery of my office.' Kieran smiled wryly. In the fourteen years since his graduation from Templemore, Kieran Clancy had arrived where he wanted to be and yet was nowhere near *what* he wanted to be. He had married the Commissioner's daughter Moya Connolly twelve years before, and had worked his way up to Detective Sergeant, as he predicted he would. There were many that derided his promotions as favours granted to the son-in-law of a Police Commissioner, but they had no idea of the hard work Kieran had put in, nor did they take the trouble to check that he had graduated top of each class he had ever attended. The rumours never bothered him.

What did bother him was that, having made it all the way to Detective Sergeant, he had now become a babysitter. He had spent the last eight years attached to Dublin Castle, and had gained the title 'Special Detective', but the only thing special about being a Special Detective as far as Kieran was concerned was that there was nothing to do. Day after day, he escorted politicians or high-ranking civil servants to and from meetings.

An elderly woman pushed the heavy door of the function room trying to get out. Kieran grabbed the brass handle and pulled it open for her. The woman smiled her thanks, nodded towards the room and remarked, 'Isn't he very good!'

'He's a wanker,' Kieran mumbled.

'I beg your pardon?' the old lady asked.

'I said thank you,' Kieran spoke out loud. The woman seemed satisfied and left. Kieran looked down the corridor. Around the corner at the bottom he saw an arm appear. It was pointed straight out and in the hand was a Webley automatic pistol. Slowly the figure of a man crept around the corner, crouched ready for action. The man made the sound of gunfire as he came towards Kieran, still half-crouched.

Kieran grinned. 'Will you put that thing away!'

The figure now stood erect; he was tall and lean with ginger hair. He pulled back the left side of his jacket to reveal a hip holster for the Webley. Spinning the gun on one finger like John Wayne, he slipped the Webley back into its holster.

'Is he still talking?' Michael Malone asked.

Kieran simply nodded. He took out a cigarette and lit it. The only time Kieran had ever asked his father-in-law for a favour was when he had been appointed as a Special Detective – he asked would it be possible to transfer Michael Malone to the same unit. The Commissioner pulled a few strings, Malone was transferred and the two men became partners. Kieran and Michael had been solid friends since Templemore. They'd been roommates there, had graduated together, and Michael had been Kieran's Best Man.

'What are you doing tonight, Kieran?' Malone asked.

'Don't know.'

'Fancy a game of snooker?' Malone tried to enthuse Kieran.

'Yes. Sure, why not.'

From inside they heard a round of applause. Kieran quickly stubbed out his cigarette, straightened his tie and buttoned his jacket.

As usual McCarthy simply came through the doors and walked past the detectives. To him they were like office furniture. The chauffeur held the door open for the Minister, who climbed into the back seat. Within seconds the limousine, followed by Kieran Clancy and Michael Malone in an unmarked detective car, left the carpark of the hotel in convoy.

* * *

Kandy Korner store, Snuggstown, 12.45pm

When Dublin Corporation decided to close the tenement buildings of Dublin and knock them down, they created in a semi-circle on the north side of the city a whole new batch of satellite towns. In some cases these were already established outlying villages that were simply expanded into towns. In other cases, as was the case in Snuggstown, a whole new town was built in what had once been green fields. Snuggstown was now the largest of the satellite towns: ninety-six thousand people living in four square miles. Although well laid out, Snuggstown had not been well planned. Now this may sound contradictory, but consider this: the new town of Snuggstown was twenty-five years old. There was no cinema in Snuggstown. There was no park in Snuggstown. There was no rail service to Snuggstown. There were only three children's playgrounds in Snuggstown. There was one police station in Snuggstown, and at any given time there were just twelve officers on duty. This meant one officer to approximately nine thousand people. So it was that Snuggstown was impossible to police. The police had, in fact, long ago become spectators to the goings-on in the place. The gangster community of Chicago, New York and the other major cities of America had learned in the 1920s that to make crime a sensitive political issue was not a good thing, so they split the cities into specific areas over which individual gangs or families had reign. This stopped inter-gang squabbling, kept crime out of the newspapers and thus off of the politicians' table. Since then most American crime has been organised like this – hence 'organised crime'.

In Snuggstown, organised crime meant Simple Simon Williams. Simon was now lord of anything illicit that moved in Snuggstown – be it drugs, protection, prostitution and the fencing of all major transactions. Simon Williams was Lord of the Manor. There were of course other drug dealers in Snuggstown, and Simon tolerated them – but only because their wholesale supply came from him. As he had predicted fifteen years previously, Simon Williams owned Snuggstown. The two henchmen who had started with him, Teddy and Bubbles Morgan, were now his lieutenants. They did Williams's running and fetching, and in return he paid them well and ignored their own little scams, such as the mickey-mouse shop protection racket they ran. It gave them a few bob, he thought, and it made them feel important.

Mind you, nothing could ever make them look important. At that moment Bubbles Morgan looked decidedly unimportant. The thirty-three-year-old man stood in a newsagent's shop reading a children's comic. He laughed aloud. His brother Teddy, standing just fifteen feet away from Bubbles at the newsagent's counter, was not laughing, and neither was the newsagent Teddy was talking to.

'Listen, Mr McArthur, it's community insurance. You pay the insurance and me and Mr Williams will make sure you don't have any trouble from the community, okay?' Teddy had a scowl on his face as he outlined the deal.

'I've had to close early every night this week. My wife has been sick, you see ...' the newsagent pleaded.

'Tell me, Mr McArthur, do I look like a fuckin' doctor?' Teddy extended his hand.

Without further comment or argument the newsagent opened the drawer of the till, picked out some notes and put them into Teddy's hand. Before he had even closed the till Teddy had put the notes in his pocket and turned his back. As he walked past his brother on the way out he had to stop and retrace his steps. He tapped Bubbles on the shoulder and signalled him to come on. Bubbles first went to put the comic down and then changed his mind. He rolled it up, stuffed it in his inside pocket, smiled at the newsagent and they both left.

St Thomas's Boxing Club, 1.00pm

St Thomas's Boxing Club had been turning young Northside Dubliners into boxers since its foundation in nineteen sixty-one. In its thirty-five-year history it had turned out six Olympic boxers. These Olympians were commemorated in the club building itself with life-size portraits down the south wall of the building. Well, actually, five life-size portraits and one larger-than-life portrait of their greatest hero, Sparrow McCabe. Over that period, of course, trainers came and trainers went. Committees changed, but unfortunately, through the usual lack of funding, very little of the decor had, though the equipment over the years had been updated.

If ever proof were needed that old boxers never die, one would just need to take a walk through the locker rooms in St Thomas's Club. There the elderly, retired boxers and trainers would gather every day for games of cards or games of chess or just to sit and talk, all of them suffering from the 'I could have been a contender' syndrome.

There had been one constant in St Thomas's Boxing Club over the past fifteen years. That constant was 'Froggy' Campbell. Every day Froggy would open the club first thing in the morning and would be the last one to leave when he locked it last thing at night. For this Froggy received no payment. Nor did he seek any. For the world of St Thomas's Boxing Club was Froggy's world. Froggy was thirty years of age, and it was believed that lack of oxygen at birth had caused Froggy's brain damage. At first everyone thought he was just deaf, but as he got older and special school followed special school, it was discovered that Froggy was trainable but not teachable. A difficult situation to explain, but best described by his mother when she would say, 'Froggy can be trained how to dress himself but he will never learn why he has to.'

A big man and perfectly healthy in every way, if a bit overweight, Froggy had the mind of a six-year-old child. He mopped out the showers, swept the gym, washed the windows, and spent his entire day shuffling from one task to another, always with a smile on his face. Froggy had two passions in his life. One was boxing, obviously. The other was his polaroid camera. The latter interest began when Froggy was sixteen years of age and he got his first camera. He'd been given it as a present from Madrid by Sparrow McCabe, the man whose portrait was bigger than any other on the club wall.

Froggy never understood what had happened to Sparrow in Spain, but he did remember that Sparrow was very sad when he returned. Still, he had taken the camera out of its box and loaded the film, showing Froggy how to work it. Froggy immediately took his very first photograph, a black-and-white head-and-shoulder shot of a very sad Sparrow McCabe.

It was Sparrow who had taken Froggy to the gym for the very first time. Sparrow had often met the retarded boy, then only fifteen years of age, as he walked to the gym. Every day the boy would smile and say, 'Hello.' And one day Sparrow stopped to talk to him. It had been a strange conversation, for at that time Froggy's vocabulary revolved around four words: Yes, Thank you, Mammy, and of course, Hello.

Sparrow was in training every day then, and he would

call to Froggy's house at the same time each day, and with Froggy's mother's permission take him by the hand down to the gym. Sparrow would be the last to leave, so he would lock up, take Froggy by the hand and walk him back home. After six months of this, Froggy began to make his own way to the gym. And because the pattern had been set, he would insist on being the last to leave the building.

Nowadays Sparrow trained only two or three times a week – and one couldn't really call it training, it was more of a work-out. But this didn't break Froggy's routine; it was easier for his mother to let him go to the gym every day than to try to un-train him.

Today was one of Sparrow's work-out days. Froggy was sweeping around the ring, for the tenth time, and all the while his eyes never left Sparrow McCabe, who was working-out on a punch-bag. Froggy was dressed in ill-fitting boxer shorts and vest, ordinary street shoes and socks, and had his latest polaroid camera hanging around his neck. His camera had been updated four times. This latest one even spoke to him. Just as he pressed the button a little voice would say, 'Watch the birdie!' Where the other three had been bought over the years by Sparrow, this latest one was a Christmas present from all the boxers who used the gym.

Froggy laid his brush against the edge of the ring and shuffled over to where Sparrow was now furiously working the bag. He lifted his camera. Snap and flash. There was a whirring sound as the camera spit out its photo. Waving it like a fan, Froggy shuffled towards the locker-room, past two older men playing chess. Both players had been boxers for years and looked like they'd been hit in the face by the same frying pan, their features identically flat. Just as Froggy passed, one of them made a move. 'What kind of a fuckin' move was that?' demanded one of the men watching the game. 'What would you know?' the one who'd made the move asked. 'I know this much, if I was the king on your board I'd be chargin' you with fuckin' treason.' The men laughed, but all this meant nothing to Froggy.

Oblivious to it all, Froggy made his way to the lockers. He opened the door of his own locker and placed the new photograph of Sparrow on top of piles and piles of photographs. Froggy had kept every photograph he had ever taken. Froggy then went to the showers and turned one on. He checked that there was soap in the soap tray. Then carefully laid a large towel outside the door of the shower for Sparrow. He whipped up a smaller towel and headed back to Sparrow.

Back at the punch-bag, Sparrow was working furiously. He threw a right-left-right combination. His body weaved right and left, his stance continually changing as the bag swung back and forth. Perspiration was running down his face and down his back and shoulders. Each punch of the bag was punctuated by a grunt. In his mind Sparrow heard the crowd scream. He threw a stiff right into the middle of the bag – and saw the Spaniard stagger away. He heard Molloy scream from the corner, 'Finish it now, finish it now.' As tears began to stream from his eyes, he jabbed the bag twice and threw a right hook. He saw his father, now deceased, standing and shouting, 'Yes Sparrow, yes Sparrow, this is it.' Sparrow stopped. With the suspension rope squeaking the bag swung from side to side. Sparrow stood, frozen, in front of it. Slowly he extended his hands and steadied the bag. Slowly he raised his right hand to his mouth and bit at the velcro on the mit. He repeated the action with the other hand and tossed the mits on the floor beneath the bag. With his head down he began to make his way to the locker room.

He was stopped on the way by Froggy. 'Will we box now, Sparrow? Come on, I box yeh!' Froggy's voice was enthusiastic.

Sparrow tried to fob him off. All around them were other boxers who had been training or working-out. They began to wind down and smile over at the two men, knowing what was coming. The Froggy-versus-Sparrow bouts had become a ritual of Sparrow's work-out days. Sparrow didn't feel like it tonight, but then he looked into Froggy's face: he was so excited, his eyes dancing in his head. Sparrow smiled and put his hand on Froggy's shoulder.

'Okay then, come on, Froggy – yeh killer!'

'Ooo ... gonna knock you fuckin' block off, Spawoo!' was Froggy's cry as he quickly made his way to the ring. The two men climbed into the ring and interrupted two sparring boxers. The training all around the gym stopped and the boys and men gathered around. Two trainers, Duffy and Flynn, hopped into the ring to be Froggy's seconds, and in the other corner one of the young boxers helped Sparrow on with his gloves. Froggy sat on the stool in the corner as if preparing for a world title fight. Flynn helped him on with his gloves, and while doing this he spoke to Froggy.

'Froggy, listen, this is important. Never smoke in the cinema – and close the cover before striking.'

Froggy looked up into Flynn's face and nodded. 'Okay, boss.'

Now Duffy joined in. 'Froggy, never piss while the train is stopped in the station.'

Froggy looked at Flynn. 'Okay, boss.'

Someone hit the bell and the two boxers rose to their feet. Just as Froggy was about to make his way out of the corner, Flynn called after him.

'Oh – and Froggy.'

Froggy spun around quickly to look at Flynn. 'Yes, boss?'

'Knock his fuckin' block off!' Flynn imparted this last bit of coaching with a smile and a wink.

Froggy smiled back. 'Okay, boss.'

The fighters met in the middle. They touched gloves, the ringsiders now beginning to cheer for Froggy. Froggy began to hop around the ring, hinting at the origin of his nickname.

'Yer goin' down, Froggy. I've got yeh this time, man. Yeh ain't got a chance, man.' Sparrow pretended to be angry.

'Knock yer fuckin' block off!' Froggy returned.

The mock fight began. Sparrow pretended to, but never actually threw a punch. Froggy was throwing awkward punches that landed on Sparrow, but were completely harmless. Eventually, as Froggy began to work up a sweat, he swung a wide right that caught Sparrow on the shoulder. Sparrow staggered and hit the canvas. Flynn jumped into the ring and began the count. Froggy was still hopping around the ring. The ringsiders joined in the count with Flynn.

'Seven – eight – nine – he's out!' They all began to shout and cheer and clap, and Froggy danced around the ring like the world champion, the ringsiders slapping his gloves and giving him the thumbs-up sign. Sparrow staggered back to his corner, smiling. Froggy shuffled over to Sparrow's corner.

'Hard luck, Spawoo. Maybe tomowoo?' he consoled him.

The youngster in the corner tugged the gloves off Sparrow's hands. Sparrow stood and put his arm around Froggy's shoulder.

'I've been saying that for fifteen years now, Froggy, but you're just too good, Froggy, you're just too good!' The two men hugged and everybody went back to training. Once again, Sparrow headed for the locker room, exchanging greetings with some of the other boxers and the older men.

One of the old men called out, 'Sparrow, have yeh heard about old Eddie dyin' on his holidays in the Isle of Man?'

'Yeh, I heard that, Tom,' said Sparrow. 'A bit of bad luck! Eddie was a good auld skin.'

'They're flyin' him home at the weekend. The funeral's Monday morning at eleven o'clock in St John's church.'

'Yeh, I know, Tom. Me and Eileen will be there.'

'Good man, Sparrow, you're a good man.' The older man rubbed his hand across Sparrow's shoulders with genuine warmth and finished with the customary slap on the neck.

Sparrow headed for the shower. Like a mischievous little child, Froggy sneaked into the shower area, tiptoed up to Sparrow's shower and aimed the camera into the cubicle. Click, flash, whirr. Froggy ran away giggling. Passing the group of old men he said, 'I got picture of Spawoo's willie.'

'Oh yeh? Well, why don't you get it enlarged for him, son?' answered one of them. The locker room burst into laughter.

In the shower cubicle Sparrow stood with his arms

spread-eagled up against the wall as the steaming water rolled down his face. He had his eyes closed. In the background he heard the laughter of the old men. Sparrow wasn't laughing. He wasn't looking forward to this funeral tomorrow, he hated funerals. In the last few years he had attended so many, two of which broke his heart – his mother's and his father's. Within a year of the fight in Madrid, Sparrow's mother Rita had died from cancer. Macker was never the same after the triple blow of losing his granddaughter, his dreams in Madrid, and then his wife within a year. He died four years later, some say of a broken heart. Sparrow didn't know if that was true but he often felt guilty for giving up boxing professionally immediately after Madrid. From that day on Macker had never had an opportunity or a reason to whip out his penis again.

***

Main Street, Snuggstown, 1.45pm

Kieran Clancy had his elbow resting on the window of the car and leaned his head against his hand, using only one hand, his left, to drive the police car. They'd been tailing the Minister's limousine for thirty-five or forty minutes now. The Minister was heading, Kieran assumed, back to Dáil Eireann – assumed, because the Minister never said where he was going, so they just tailed him. Detective Malone sat quietly in the passenger seat. It was sunny for December and on the footpath some girls had ventured out in mini skirts. Malone watched them all with a smile on his face.

'I love this job,' Malone commented out of the blue.

'I hate this job,' Clancy retorted.

Michael turned his full attention to Clancy. 'Kieran Clancy! I never thought I'd hear the day when you'd say you hate being a copper.'

'No, no, I didn't mean that. I've always wanted to be a policeman. I just hate this – babysitting these shit-heads.'

'Now, wait a minute, Kieran, it's an important job. After all, he is a Minister.'

'Minister for crapology. Let me tell you, Michael, the only person who might shoot that fella is one of the gobshites that voted for him.' As Clancy said this he pointed straight ahead at the ministerial limousine, and Michael's gaze followed. The left indicator went on and it began to pull in. The police car followed suit.

'Now what's he up to?' They saw the chauffeur climb out of the driver's door and quickly make his way around to the Minister's door. He held it open for the Minister, who left the car hurriedly and entered a doorway. 'What in God's name ...?' Clancy was mumbling as he climbed out of his car. He didn't have to ask – it was written all over the chauffeur's face. 'He's gone for a ... a rub, says he's a bit stiff,' the chauffeur explained, nodding towards the doorway. Clancy turned and looked at the sign over the doorway. The tacky sign read 'Medusa Massage'.

Clancy threw his eyes in the air and returned to his car, shaking his head. Michael was now out of the car and waiting for Clancy's return. Kieran took his packet of cigarettes from his pocket, lit one, turned his collar up and leaned back against the car.

'So what's up?' Michael asked.

With the smoking cigarette between his lips Kieran

nodded towards the doorway. 'Your Minister pal has gone for a wank!'

'What? Off who?' Michael asked.

Kieran stared at him, one of those stares that says, Why are you asking such a stupid question?

'Off his chauffeur ... in there, you idiot!' Kieran again nodded to the doorway.

'You mean that's a ...'

Clancy simply nodded again.

'Well, my God! I didn't even know that place existed,' exclaimed Michael slowly, careful not to let Clancy see him jot the phone number of the Medusa Massage Parlour on the palm of his hand. 'And how much would a wank be?' Michael wondered.

Clancy gave him that look again. 'Are you asking me to quote you? How the hell would I know?'

Michael didn't pursue it. Clancy threw his cigarette on the footpath and stood on it. He dug his hands deep into his pockets and stamped his feet to keep warm. As he did this he glanced around at the main street.

'God almighty, this place is desperate!'

'It's a kip, all right! I'm glad we're not stationed out here in Snuggstown.'

'Yes, Michael, that would be terrible – we might have to pretend to be policemen.'

'You're in great form, aren't you?'

The doorway of a building across the street opened and a man stepped out. His hair was thin on top, and he had a moustache; he was wearing denim trousers and a bomber jacket. He was carrying a sports bag. Kieran watched him as he walked towards them up the street. His face seemed vaguely familiar. Kieran frowned, then the dawning of recognition made his eyebrows rise.

'Look! Isn't that Sparrow McCabe over there, Michael?'

Michael turned and looked at the figure walking in their direction on the far side of the street.

'It is, indeed. God, he was some boxer.'

'He sure was.' They watched as Sparrow walked a short way down the street and inserted a key into the door of a black Jaguar.

'I wonder did he take a dive that time in Spain?' Michael asked Clancy.

Clancy continued to watch Sparrow. 'He must be doing all right now, driving a Jag.'

'That's not his.'

Kieran now looked at Michael. 'How do you know?'

'I know because before you got me this cushy number, I was in Traffic. The Jag belongs to that scumbag Simon Williams – Simple Simon. He runs Snuggstown.' Michael turned and nodded towards Medusa's. 'He probably owns that place. Sparrow drives for him. He has done for about the last six years.'

As Sparrow climbed into the Jaguar the two men watched him with interest, but were interrupted by the Minister as he exited from the massage parlour. Without a word to either his chauffeur or his bodyguards, the Minister climbed straight back into the ministerial car. The two detectives got into their car and Kieran started the engine, his eyes still fixed on Sparrow. As they set off down the street, they drove past the Jaguar. Kieran Clancy stared at Sparrow. Sparrow met his stare and frowned. The first meeting of these two men was over. It would not be the last.

CHAPTER SEVEN

Thursday, 5 December
The McCabe home, Snuggstown West, 9.45pm

Sparrow McCabe lived in a two-bedroomed terraced house in Meadowmist housing estate. Although this area was still referred to as the 'new estate', it was actually twelve years old, but hung on to its name because it was the final phase of the Snuggstown West housing plan. Just two years after their marriage, Sparrow and Eileen had applied for one of the new houses. Less than a year later they had moved in. The design of the houses was simple. Upstairs there was one large bedroom in which Eileen and Sparrow slept. Next to it was a bathroom and toilet. At that moment Sparrow was standing at the door of the second, smaller bedroom. Inside this room lay the family jewel. After the tragic loss of her daughter in Madrid, it was seven years before Eileen gave birth again. The pregnancy was a tense and tortured time for both of them. When the boy was born he was greeted with a huge sigh of relief rather than open joy. Eileen named him Michael, after her father, but this had quickly been shortened to Mickey. As the boy grew into a seven-year-old scamp, the name suited him perfectly.

Sparrow pushed Mickey's bedroom door open softly. The light from the single bulb on the landing spilled in. Mickey's room was typical of a seven-year-old's bedroom. His clothes were scattered along the floor where he had tossed them, for like most seven-year-olds he undressed on his way to the bed. Quietly Sparrow gathered up the clothes and folded them. He picked up the child's things as well – a football and a tiny TV with a computer game console attached to it. The monitor was on and Sparrow clicked it off. The walls were adorned with various posters showing the diversity of Mickey's interests: Hulk Hogan, the Irish football team, various players in various poses from Aston Villa FC, and a huge Spice Girls poster reflecting Mickey's anticipation of future adolescence rather than his musical taste.

On Mickey's bedside table were two framed photographs. One was of the boy himself in football gear, holding a ball. He was laughing and covered from head to toe in mud. Sparrow picked it up and smiled as he looked at this little bundle of energy. He then quietly replaced it beside the photo of himself, a black-and-white one, in full boxing regalia. Sparrow lost his smile.

Mickey was sound asleep but still wearing the headphones of his walkman, so Sparrow leaned over and gently lifted the headphones from the boy's head. He smiled down at his son lovingly, and bending over him placed a gentle kiss on his forehead. 'Goodnight, Mickey the Gick!'

Sparrow made his way downstairs, on the way tossing Mickey's clothes into the washbasket in the bathroom. He flicked on the kettle, then went to the fireplace. It was freezing cold outside, so he heaped some more coal onto the fire, to have the room nice and warm for Eileen when she returned from bingo. Thursday night was bingo night and Eileen made it her night out with her mother, Dolly. Over the hearth the entire wall was covered with photographs, framed press clippings and other memorabilia from Sparrow's boxing years. Eileen called this Sparrow's Wall.

The kettle began to dance. Sparrow hurried to the kitchen counter and switched it off. He tossed a tea bag into a mug, then two sugars, finally adding the scalding water. As the tea 'brewed' in the mug he made himself some sandwiches. Within minutes Sparrow was closing the kitchen door with his leg, and holding the tea in one hand, a sandwich in the other and another sandwich in his mouth, he settled himself into his armchair.

He reached down to the floor beside his chair and his hand found the remote control. Then like a gunslinger he began to flick through the channels until he found Sky Sports. A handsome sports announcer with plastic features announced: *'Coming up next here on Sky Sports we have Fight Night, tonight featuring the European Heavyweight Title Fight between Karim Smith of London, and Spain's Enzo Vala. That's after the break.'* As an advert began, Sparrow's eyes drifted to the fire flickering in the hearth, then up to the wall over the mantelpiece. He noticed that one of the frames hanging there was crooked. It was a press cutting, with the headline: 'McCABE LOSES OUT'. As if from a distance he heard Jimmy Magee's voice boom out:

'The little Irishman is going to work, a left, a right, he's pushing the Spaniard towards the ropes. I see blood coming from the cut in Sparrow's eye but it's not stopping him! Another cruncher

from the Irish champ to the body. Surely, it's all over now. The Spaniard's guard comes down ...'

How many times had he replayed that commentary? Sparrow asked himself.

The 'ding, ding, ding' of the bell startled Sparrow back to reality. The fight on television was about to begin. He turned to go back to his chair and saw Eileen standing in the kitchen doorway watching him. She removed her satin headscarf and her blond hair fell to her shoulders. Even after fifteen years of marriage Sparrow thought she was still beautiful. Quite beautiful.

'Fighting the Spaniard again?' Eileen asked flatly.

'Yeh.'

'And who won?'

'He did.'

'Again?'

'Yeh. Again.'

Eileen went to the kitchen counter and flicked the kettle on. 'Was Mickey okay?'

Sparrow was settling back down in the armchair. 'Yeh, he was grand, he's asleep. How was bingo?'

'Okay. D'yeh want some more tea?'

'Yeh please. This is gone cold.'

Eileen walked to Sparrow's armchair, took his mug and made her way back to the sink. She poured out the cold tea and rinsed the mug out. While she was wiping it with the dishcloth Sparrow stared at her. Her body language told him that she was not a happy girl. But she'd not been a happy girl for many years now.

'How's your mother?' Sparrow tried by way of conversation.

Eileen again answered without turning, still busying herself making tea. 'Oh yeh know, still the same, still giving out.' She brought Sparrow's tea over to him. As she placed it on the arm of the chair she looked into his face. 'She says I should leave you.'

Sparrow looked in her eyes, and saw they were sad. 'Maybe she's right, Eileen.'

They looked at each other.

Eileen's ears pinned back and her nose flared. 'Sparrow, will yeh fuck off!' She began to take off her coat and leave the room at the same time.

Sparrow jumped up and caught her arm, but she pulled away from him.

'I'm sorry, Eileen, I was only messing. Really love, I'm sorry.'

Eileen looked into Sparrow's eyes and spoke angrily. 'Sparrow, don't even *say* things like that, not even as a joke. Sometimes I don't know with you.' He could see she was holding back tears. She pointed to the mantelpiece. 'You fight that fuckin' Spaniard every day. And every day you lose! That was years ago. Throw the fuckin' punch, Sparrow, for God's sake, and let us get on with our lives!'

Sparrow took Eileen in his arms. 'It's not like that, love,' he began. 'I'm just remembering –'

Eileen pushed him away. 'It is like that, Sparrow. You just can't forget it. The fight is over, Sparrow. You lost. I'm warning you, Sparrow McCabe, we've had just about as much of this shit as we can take. Mickey adores you and as much as I love you too one of these days you're going to look into your corner and we won't be there! That'll give you something else to blame on the Spaniard!'

Sparrow turned away and leaned on the fireplace with his back to his wife. The memorabilia of the wall seemed stark to him now. Sparrow in action – press clippings: 'McCABE, THE BEST I'VE EVER SEEN'; 'YOUNGEST EVER NATIONAL CHAMPION'; 'TEN IN A ROW FOR THE SPARROW'.

Eileen went over to him and spoke to his back. Waving her hand across the memorabilia, she said, 'Turn it around, Sparrow. All of this must count for something – there are people out there that remember the best of Sparrow McCabe.'

Sparrow spun around to face her. He was perspiring and the pain was obvious in his face. 'The loser,' he blurted out.

'For Christ's sake, Sparrow, you lost one fight! What about the fifty you won?'

'Yeh, what about them? I'll tell yeh, Eileen, I'll tell yeh about them. They count for nothing! Eileen, before I left for Spain, your brother-in-law offered me a sales manager's job. Sales fuckin' manager.' Sparrow spat this out.

'And he still wants you to work for him!' Eileen's voice had gone up a pitch.

Sparrow smirked and slowly sank into his armchair. 'Yeh, as a security man. What happened to the sales manager? I'll tell you what happened, Eileen, he's still lying on the canvas in Madrid because he couldn't finish the job. He hadn't got the bottle. Don't yeh see, Eileen, nobody wants a loser!'

But Eileen wasn't giving up. 'The only one in this house that thinks you're a loser is you! And what's wrong with being a security man, anyway? It would be better than me sitting here worrying every day if you're going to come home. Or if I'll have to explain to Mickey why his father is in prison. Or worse – dead! And will Simon Williams give a shit? Will he?'

Sparrow jumped to a standing position, not to continue the argument but because behind Eileen young Mickey was standing in the doorway, rubbing his eyes sleepily.

Eileen turned to see what Sparrow was looking at, and still hyped up from her outburst, she turned on the boy and shouted, 'What are you doing up?'

Startled, Mickey began to sob. 'I had a nightmare!'

Sparrow pushed past Eileen and hugged the boy into his body.

'It's all right, Mickey boy, dreams can't hurt yeh!' Sparrow began to usher the boy out of the room towards the stairs. 'Come on, Mickey, I'll lie down with you for a while.'

'Are you going to prison, Dad?' the boy asked in a scared voice.

'No, son, I'm not going to prison. Mammy's just trying to make a point.' Sparrow laughed.

When the two had left the room, Eileen walked slowly to the mantelpiece, tears of frustration in her eyes. She looked at the framed picture of the fight in Madrid and then in an outburst of tears punched the picture, shattering the glass.

CHAPTER EIGHT

Monday, 9 December
St John's Church, 11.00am

Eileen and Sparrow made their way down the aisle of the church towards the coffin. Eileen glanced around at the large gathering that had come to see old Eddie off. There was a great number of old and young boxers; Eileen had never seen such a large collection of battered ears and noses in one place.

'Are these all boxers?' she whispered to Sparrow.

'Yeh. If you see a fella here with two ears he's a fuckin' sissy,' Sparrow replied.

Eileen dug her elbow into Sparrow's side. 'Sparrow, watch your language in the church.' But she giggled all the same.

There was to be no requiem mass, just a simple sending off and blessing of the coffin. Sparrow and Eileen took their places, about ten rows from the front of the church. The priest in full vestments stood at the head of the coffin facing the congregation. To one side was Eddie's widow, dressed suitably in black and sniffling. On the other side stood

Eddie's son, looking awkward. The priest genuflected at the altar and descended to the coffin, where an altar boy proffered a small brass bucket containing holy water on a tray. Beside the bucket was a brass rod with a sphere on the end of it. The priest dipped the sphere in the bucket and made the Sign of the Cross over the coffin with it. The blessed water landed silently on old Eddie's coffin.

The priest then handed the sphere to Eddie's son. The altar boy went to Eddie's son's side. Slightly puzzled, the son dipped the sphere in the bucket and made the Sign of the Cross, looking at the priest for approval. The priest nodded and smiled. He handed the rod back to the priest.

The priest turned to Eddie's widow whose face was buried in her handkerchief. He tapped her gently on the shoulder and handed her the rod, while the altar boy moved to her side. She was completely puzzled. She looked at the rod, but didn't take it from the priest. The priest offered it again, more forcefully. She took it. She stared at it for a moment or two. The priest straightened himself and joined his hands in front of his chest. Eddie's widow held the sphere up to her lips and began to make a speech:

'I'd like to thank you all for coming here today. Eddie was a good husband and will be very proud to see so many of his friends coming to his funeral!' She held the rod and sphere as Tom Jones would hold a microphone.

The reaction of the congregation was mixed. Some were embarrassed, some laughed under their breath. Sparrow and Eileen grinned at each other, then to relieve the now-awkward silence Sparrow began to clap. Everybody joined in. The widow smiled. Puzzled at first, the priest then smiled and clapped along too. He put his hand over to receive the rod back from the widow, but she held onto it. 'Eh – thank you all very much!' The widow now smiled a self-satisfied smile, completing her task with relish.

* * *

The Clancy home – 11.15am

Moya Clancy was preparing a late breakfast for Kieran and the girls. Her two beautiful young daughters – Claire, seven, and Mary, four – sat at the breakfast table, their faces deep into their cereal bowls. Moya shuttled between the sink, the cooker and the fridge. She seemed agitated. It had taken three house-moves over the years of their marriage to find the home that Moya really liked. This was it. There was plenty of space for the children to play in. Good neighbours. And, most important of all, a first-class kitchen and large dining room for entertaining. Cooking and entertaining were two of Moya Clancy's passions, something she had inherited from her mother and a talent that was essential for the wife of every ambitious policeman.

The children heard the footsteps of their father coming down the stairs. They looked at each other and smiled. Seconds later the kitchen door burst open and Kieran stepped in, singing.

'Who put the bop in the bop do wah de bop?' He stopped and waited, pointing at the children.

'Who put the ram in the ram a lam a ding bam?' the children sang back, and all three laughed.

'Good morning, my princesses!' Kieran greeted his ladies.

'Good morning, father of the princesses,' Claire replied formally as if reciting Shakespeare.

Kieran took his seat at the breakfast table and Moya placed a big fry of sausages, rashers and grilled tomatoes in front of him. As she poured out his tea she seemed distracted.

'I do wish you'd stop this carry-on, Kieran. The children will have to learn that the table is for eating and not for fun and games. It's difficult for me to teach them that if you arrive in here every morning like Jerry Lee Lewis!' She put the teapot down and went back to the cooker.

'You're quite right, love, and I'm sorry,' Kieran replied, then he winked at the children and they both winked back.

'Wait a minute – how come you two aren't at school?' Kieran asked the girls.

'It's a Holy Day, Daddy. And after mass, Mum is taking us into town to see Santa Claus!' Claire answered. Young Mary was looking at Claire all the time she spoke and as she said the name Santa Claus, Mary stiffened and squinted her eyes with excitement. Kieran laughed. Moya returned to the table with a cup of tea for herself and began to shoo the kids away.

'Right, girls, come on, up you go, tidy your rooms and brush your teeth. Go on, off with you now, off you go!'

The children left their places, kissed their father and then charged up the stairs, shrieking with excitement.

Kieran began to eat. 'They're madly excited!' he commented, eyeing Moya and knowing something was up. Moya confirmed this by simply staring at her mug and running her finger around the rim. 'So, are you going to tell me what's up?' Kieran asked.

'What do you mean?' Moya said nonchalantly.

'Moya, we've been having breakfast together now for years, and every time you run your finger around the rim of the cup, it means you have something on your mind. So what is it?'

Quickly Moya took her finger away, a little flustered. 'Daddy rang this morning,' she said flatly.

Kieran dropped his head and began to concentrate again on his breakfast. 'Oh, I see. And what does the Commissioner have to say to his darling daughter today?'

Before Moya answered she took a packet of cigarettes out of her handbag and lit one. Kieran's eyebrows rose – he had never seen Moya smoke in the morning. Moya took a drag from her cigarette and slowly blew out the smoke. Unconsciously, she began to run her finger around the rim of her mug again.

'Daddy told me you applied for the Special Task Force again!'

Kieran didn't look at her. 'Did he now? And did he say what reason he's going to give this time for turning me down?'

Moya shot a glance at Kieran. 'He's only trying to look after us, Kieran.'

'Well, I don't want to be looked after. I didn't join the police force to spend my life escorting politicians to meetings. I want to be a policeman. A real fucking policeman!'

'Mind your language, Kieran, the girls will hear you.' Moya glanced at the door. Kieran stood up and went to put his plate in the sink. 'Well, thank God someone hears me because you certainly don't, Moya.'

He came back to join her at the table. 'Let me be my own man, Moya.' He seemed very agitated. 'Look, Moya,' he said, 'I know your father means well, and I know you don't want to have to worry. But I'll tell you, love, if he blocks me this time I'll ... I'll crack up!' Kieran slumped down into his seat at the table and held his head in his hands.

There was silence between them now. Moya poured them both more tea. She took another drag from her cigarette. She didn't look at Kieran.

'I asked him to give it to you. Not to block it.'

Kieran closed his eyes. 'You did? Oh thank you, love.'

'Merry Christmas.' Moya began to cry.

Kieran hugged her. 'It'll be all right, love. You'll see, it'll be all right.'

* * *

Kavanagh's pub – near Glasnevin Cemetery, 1.20pm

Old Eddie would have been proud of his funeral party. It was a very merry affair, as is the custom for funerals in Ireland. Eileen and her mother Dolly were standing talking to four other women. They were laughing and giggling. Obviously woman-talk. Taking a sip from her drink, Eileen glanced around the room to see where Sparrow was. He was standing over at the bar listening to the stories of two older boxers. The old fellow at Sparrow's left was showing him a jab and a right-cross. Sparrow nodded dutifully. Eileen thought she felt something touch her behind, like something leaning against her bottom. Suddenly she was pinched. She spun around to see who the offender was. The broad, burly, pugnacious-looking man gaping at her was Teddy Morgan. Eileen's smile turned to a scowl. 'Would you mind keeping your hands to yourself,' she said through clenched teeth.

'Now, now, Eileen, you know you want me,' Teddy sneered back at her.

Dolly joined in the attack. 'Leave her alone, yeh big bollix.' Dolly Coffey did not mince her words.

Teddy slowly raised his arm and gently stroked Eileen's cheek. 'Still Mammy's little girl, eh Eileen?'

Dolly wasn't giving up. 'Here, why don't you bring in your brother and double your IQ to fuckin' six!' The other women laughed.

Teddy didn't like being laughed at, and he turned his attention to Mrs Coffey. 'Yeh have a big mouth, Missus,' he said nastily.

The women around Dolly went quiet. But Dolly didn't back off – in fact she leaned towards Teddy. 'Big enough to bite yer fuckin' head off.'

Suddenly Sparrow came over. He stood between Mrs Coffey, Eileen and Teddy. Although shorter by far than Teddy, he still squared up to him. When Sparrow spoke, his voice was quiet and even. 'Have you a problem, Teddy?'

'Don't give me this macho shit, Sparrow. I might just take offence and break your fuckin' neck!'

'Then you better get the neck on its own, Teddy.' Sparrow stared straight into Teddy's eyes. Eileen wanted to take Sparrow by the hand and pull him away, but she knew better. Any sudden movement now might just be the spark that'd cause the explosion. The two men stood looking at each other. The entire pub had gone quiet. Bottles were taken from the tables and held by people's sides. Old boxers were ready to move into action if required. Teddy slowly glanced around the room and the expressions on all the faces told him he had no friends here. He backed down. 'Just get the keys of the car, Sparrow. Simon wants the collecting done by four o'clock.'

Sparrow's eyes didn't leave Teddy and the pitch of his voice didn't change. 'I'll follow you out.'

Teddy turned and sneered at Mrs Coffey and gave Eileen a suggestive wink as he left. The general conversation rose again.

Sparrow turned to Eileen. 'See you at about half-five, love. Are you all right?'

'I'm grand, Sparrow. You mind yourself, love!'

He kissed her softly and into her ear whispered, 'I will – I'm sorry about last night, love.' They smile at each other, and a simple wink from Eileen told Sparrow that he was forgiven for his suggestion that they might separate. Sparrow tossed the keys in the air and left the pub.

* * *

Snuggstown Shopping Centre, 3.45pm

The black Jaguar was parked outside the video shop. Sparrow sat in the driver's seat reading a newspaper. The street was decked out with Christmas lights and all the shops festooned with decorations. Sparrow was half-reading the newspaper and half-mulling over what he would get Eileen for Christmas. The two Morgan brothers came out of the video shop, laughing, and climbed into the back of the

77

Jaguar. Sparrow tucked his paper between the seats and started the car. He put on the left-hand indicator and pulled out into traffic, checking his rear-view mirror as he did. In the mirror he saw Teddy rip open an envelope and extract cash from it. Sparrow closed his eyes.

When Sparrow took the job as driver for Simon Williams he knew exactly what Simple Simon did for a living, and he knew exactly what he would be doing for Simple Simon – driving him here, driving him there, and driving Teddy and Bubbles wherever Simple Simon told them they had to be at any given time. He knew Simon Williams ran the drugs, prostitution and racketeering scenes in Snuggstown, but Sparrow absolved himself by continually telling himself, I only drive the car – just like the piano player who takes no responsibility for the singer's performance. The truth was that Sparrow had never broken the law in his life and he had made it clear to Williams when he took the job that he was not getting involved in anything like that. And in the six years he had worked for Williams he had never been asked to do anything other than drive the car and mind his own business.

'Right, that's the last one!' Teddy said as he tucked the money in his inside pocket. 'We'll pick the boss up from his mother-in-law's, and then it's home to Snuggstown.' Teddy spoke to Sparrow's eyes in the rear-view mirror. Sparrow simply nodded back.

Within fifteen minutes they had arrived at old Mrs Plunkett's. She lived in a Dublin flat complex. As the Jaguar pulled into the courtyard of the tenement flats it looked decidedly out of place, yet nobody took a blind bit of notice of it. Sparrow applied the handbrake and honked the horn twice. Within moments a ground-floor door opened and a man and a woman emerged. Dressed to kill in his tan cashmere crombie coat and brown trilby hat, Simon Williams made his way to the car. If Simon was the most feared man in Snuggstown, the person coming behind him was surely the most feared woman, Simon's wife, Angie. Angie was a pretty woman, who wore too much make up. She had a reasonably good figure and wore expensive clothes, the best that money could buy. Whatever Angie wanted, Angie got. She had short blond hair and an even shorter fuse. Many's the man who was found unconscious in an alley because he had upset Angie. And it didn't take too much to upset Angie – a taxi driver simply looking at her the 'wrong way' could find himself a week later with a broken arm. Sparrow worried about Angie. He didn't ever want to upset her. She reminded him of the kids at the end of his road who kept pitbull dogs; you were all right unless you upset them, but they would never tell you what it was that upset them. So Sparrow went out of his way not to talk to Angie and not to make eye-contact with her if he could help it.

Teddy jumped from the passenger seat in the front of the car and helped Angie put her shopping bags into the boot. After seeing Simon and Angie safe into the back seat he climbed back into the front beside Sparrow. Williams looked every inch the businessman to Sparrow as he eyed him in the rear-view mirror.

'Home, Mr Williams?' Sparrow asked. Simon was waving out the window at his mother-in-law and didn't turn around. 'Home, Sparrow, like a good man, and don't spare the horses!'

Angie leaned forward and poked Sparrow in the neck. 'Take it easy, you, there's china in them bags in the boot,' she warned.

Slowly the Jaguar pulled away from the flats and headed for Snuggstown. Ten minutes later they passed the Fairy Well which marked the city boundary with Snuggstown. Sparrow smiled towards the Fairy Well and said aloud, 'Hello, fairies!' as he did every time he passed the well. Years ago his mother had told him that if he didn't say hello to the fairies every time he passed them they would not be good to him. And like all good Irish Catholics, Sparrow was superstitious. Simon smiled and Angie looked to heaven. The car was quiet; there was no conversation.

To break the silence, Sparrow spoke to Simon. 'I see the Falcon has opened up again, boss!'

'The Falcon? The Falcon Inn? When?' Simon asked with a frown on his face.

'Last night, a new owner. A northern fella. The word is he's IRA,' Sparrow said.

Teddy wasn't convinced. 'IRA, me bollix! Some stone-thrower opens a pub and every gobshite in the area is callin' him IRA!'

'Last night?' It was as if Simon hadn't even heard Teddy speak. 'I didn't hear anything about that.'

Angie now joined the conversation and as always was the antagoniser. 'They shouldn't do that without consulting you, love. No fuckin' respect, that's what that is. No fuckin' respect.'

There was silence in the car for a few moments.

'Sparrow!' Simon said.

Sparrow looked in his mirror at Simon. Simon's expression had completely changed. It had got darker. 'Yeh, boss?'

'Take a right at the dairy. I'll go up and introduce myself to this – new owner!'

In a reflex action that comes from years of boxing, Sparrow's stomach muscles tightened and tiny beads of perspiration popped out behind his ears. He had what his mother would have called 'a foreboding'.

* * *

Garda Headquarters, Dublin, 4.00pm

The unmarked detectives' car was parked outside the Harcourt Hotel. Detective Michael Malone sat in the passenger seat, with his wage packet on his lap, reading his pay slip. He frowned when he read the amount of tax deducted this week.

'The bastards!' he exclaimed, not caring that somebody had to pay his wages. He was alone and speaking to himself. He wondered what was delaying Kieran, and glanced out the passenger window just in time to see him leave the Garda Headquarters across the street.

Kieran made his way over. He had a broad grin on his face. When he climbed into the driver's seat there was an air of excitement about him.

'So, what's up?' Michael asked.

Kieran half-turned in the seat to face Michael. 'Good news and bad news,' Kieran announced. He saw the puzzled look on Michael's face. 'I've been transferred to the Special Task Force. I've just had a chat inside and they told me I'm taking over as Detective Sergeant of the Serious Crime Squad in Snuggstown.'

Michael's mouth opened. 'God almighty, Kieran! That is bad news.'

'No, Michael, that's the good news!' Kieran smiled broadly.

'So, what's the bad news?'

Kieran leaned conspiratorially towards Michael. Instinctively Michael leaned towards Kieran. Kieran gave Michael a little poke with his finger on the shoulder. 'The bad news is you're coming with me!'

'No way!'

'Sorry!'

'No bloody way, Kieran – you didn't!'

'I did, Michael, believe me I did! From Monday on, you and I are gonna be real coppers.'

Kieran started the car and began to drive. Two hundred yards down the road he slapped the steering wheel. 'The Series Crime Squad! Yes!' Kieran was ecstatic.

Michael Malone stared sheepishly out the passenger window. 'Oh hell!' he muttered.

* * *

The Falcon Inn, Snuggstown, 4.30pm

Fintan McCullagh, formerly of Belfast, was proud to be the new publican at the Falcon Inn pub. Built in the mid-1970s it was situated right in the middle of the west side of Snuggstown – the toughest side. Since it had opened its doors, the pub had had fifteen owners. Most went into the venture with a keen interest and came out with a nervous breakdown. Without doubt the Falcon Inn had been the roughest, toughest pub in Snuggstown. Fintan knew all this, but was undeterred, having lived in Belfast through riots, bombings and internment. He was not a man who scared easy. He had a sharp Northern Ireland accent. He had already heard the rumours that he was fronting the pub for the IRA, and frankly he did little to deter them. In fact, he used his accent to good effect.

The previous night had been his opening and the beginnings of a fight had broken out. But it hadn't reached the punch stage by the time Fintan arrived on the scene. He looked at the two men involved and simply said, 'Are ye havin' a wee problem here, gentlemen?' The two stared at each other and then at Fintan, and slowly shook their heads. 'Good,' he said. ''Cause I don't like wee problems, you see. When I come up against a wee problem I have to find a solution. Messy business, don't you know. Enjoy your drink, gentlemen.' The two men finished their drinks; there was no fight. When they were leaving, Fintan took them to one side. 'Thank you for your custom, but don't come back,' he warned them. He could tell by the looks on their faces that they wouldn't.

So if the people of Snuggstown West had decided that Fintan was connected with the IRA, and that kept peace in his pub, then so be it.

Fintan was taking advantage of the fact that it was early evening and the pub only had about five or six customers. He was standing at the end of the bar, musing over a crossword puzzle. About forty years of age, he had silvery blond hair tied in a ponytail. Behind him an open fire blazed away, throwing an orange flicker across one side of his face and body. The heat was gorgeous.

There was just one barman on duty, PJ Duff, a local lad. PJ couldn't believe his luck when the pub just around the corner from his home had reopened and he had secured a job as a barman. PJ hadn't had a steady job for three years. He was thrilled with the position, and enthusiastic too. Even though the bar was not busy, PJ was working his way along the shelves polishing the bottles. He was that kind of man – he couldn't sit still and would always find something to do. Fintan took another sip from his coffee cup and spoke a crossword clue aloud.

'Backing in to a railway. Mmm.' He was so engrossed that he barely noticed when the four people entered the lounge. The other customers noticed, however, and all but two of them left abruptly. Simon Williams, his wife Angie and the Morgan boys settled themselves at the bar. PJ wiped his hands and turned to the customers.

'What'll it be ...' PJ froze in mid-sentence. He glanced over at Fintan. But Fintan didn't even look up from his newspaper.

PJ went back to his customers. 'Hello, Mr Williams, what can I get yeh?' PJ's hands were shaking now.

'Em, three pints of Budweiser and a glass of Guinness, son,' Simon ordered.

'With blackcurrant!' Angie added.

'Eh, the Guinness with blackcurrant, son,' Simon confirmed.

PJ quickly began to get the drinks. The shaking in his hands was still there and he was perspiring with nervousness. Again he glanced at Fintan who seemed to be still engrossed in his crossword.

Simon, thanks to PJ's glances, now knew who the boss

was. He looked down the bar at Fintan as he lit a slim cigar. Taking a long, slow draw from the cigar he turned to Bubbles Morgan. 'Bubbles, go out and tell Sparrow to come in, we could do with a laugh. This place is fuckin' dead.' Bubbles nodded and left quickly.

Now Fintan looked up. His eyes met Simon's eyes. Both men stared at each other, expressionless. It was Simon who looked away as the barman placed the last of the drinks on the counter.

'That looks like a nice pint, son, well done!'

Again PJ glanced at Fintan. Fintan had turned and was walking to the CD jukebox. He inserted a coin. He flipped through the albums, mulling over his decision.

PJ, more nervous than ever now, looked at Simon, his voice trembling. 'Seven-eighty!'

'Ten, twenty, thirty! How do you play this game?' Teddy asked sarcastically.

PJ glanced nervously towards Fintan. Fintan had his back to everyone. 'The ... eh ... drink, that's the price of the drink. Seven pounds and eighty pence.'

'Well, now, that's nice to know, isn't it, Mr Williams?' Teddy said as he lifted his pint and took a swig.

'Absolutely! It's nice to keep abreast of the cost of living,' Simon replied, and he handed the glass of Guinness to Angie, who was getting excited, lusting for a fight.

Fintan now turned around and walked in behind the bar. He went up to the group.

PJ looked at him. 'I'm sorry, Mr McCullagh, it's ...'

Fintan put his hand on the young man's shoulder. 'That's fine, son, don't worry about it! You get yourself a cup of coffee and I'll look after the bar. Go on now, son, have a wee break.' Fintan straightened up a few bottles and wandered up to Simon's group.

'Good evening, gentlemen,' he said. 'Welcome to the Falcon Inn – *my* pub!'

Teddy shifted uncomfortably. Simon, mid-mouthful, stared over the rim of his glass. Then he placed his glass on the bar and smacked his lips. 'Thank you. And you're welcome to Snuggstown – *my* town!' Simon smiled.

Fintan smiled back. 'How's the drink – all right?'

Simon stared at him and waited a couple of seconds before answering. 'It's fine. In fact it's quite nice.'

'Then, perhaps you might pay for it!' Fintan said this without changing the smile on his face.

Teddy now became aggressive. 'This is Simon Williams. Mr Williams pays for nothin' in Snuggstown, never mind four poxy drinks.'

Although Teddy's voice was angry, Fintan didn't take his eyes off Simon. With an incredibly swift movement he picked up the four glasses and put them down behind the counter. He then simply walked away. As he did, he said over his shoulder, 'Good night now, gentlemen. And Merry Christmas!'

Teddy was speechless. Simon placed a restraining hand on him. Simon stared at the back of Fintan who was back at the CD machine finishing his selection.

'Easy, Teddy boy! Not here. Not now!' Simon muttered.

The door of the lounge opened and Sparrow and Bubbles came in. They were laughing. Sparrow immediately took in the Mexican stand-off, and his laugh stopped. 'Oh fuck,' he gasped under his breath. 'Shit!'

Simon addressed himself to the young barman. 'PJ – PJ Duff, isn't it?'

The young man looked up from his coffee and nodded slowly.

'Give me up those drinks, like a good man,' Simon ordered.

PJ glanced over his shoulder at Fintan. Fintan did not turn around but his broad Northern Ireland accent boomed out, 'Stay where you are, son. Drink your coffee.'

'Come on, son, you don't want to listen to that shit. Do the right thing, son,' Simon ordered again.

PJ wanted to simply burst into tears. He felt like a rope in a tug-of-war. 'Ah Jaysus, Mr Williams. I only work here,' he implored.

'Not for fuckin' long, yeh little bollix.' Teddy was glaring at PJ now.

Simon slid off the stool and slowly walked the ten or so paces to where Fintan was standing with his back to the group. Simon addressed the man's back. When he spoke his voice was calm – but you'd know it was a voice that meant business. 'I'll be back, pal. Be fuckin' assured, I'll be back!'

Fintan pressed the final button on his CD machine selection, and just before the jaunty Christmas music blared out he turned to face Simon. 'Good,' he said, 'next time bring money.'

The two men again stared at each other for some seconds, then Simon turned and walked out, followed by Angie and Teddy.

Angie, disappointed that there wasn't going to be a bust up, was goading Simon. 'The cheeky bastard, no respect – who does he think he is?' She stopped at the doorway, turned and screamed at Fintan. 'Stick your drink up your arse!' and left haughtily.

CHAPTER NINE

Thursday, 12 December

Snuggstown Police Station, 9.25am

Kieran Clancy had not expected a brass band and party balloons to greet him on his arrival at Snuggstown police station to take over as the new head of the Serious Crime Squad. But he had expected to be greeted in a civil manner. Instead, when he presented himself at the reception desk in the station he was met coldly by a ruddy-faced, country sergeant, who needed either to diet or change the size of his uniform. This was Sergeant Toddy Muldoon. After fifteen years in Snuggstown, Muldoon had things very much his own way. He liked to gamble and was a drinker. Still, this did not affect his standard of living, which was surprisingly high. Few knew how he managed this on a sergeant's salary, and those who did know were not saying. Kieran introduced himself as the new head of the Serious Crime Squad and asked where his office was. He expected to get more than the jerk of a thumb and a simple two-word reply: 'Down there.'

The Sergeant looked him up and down, then turned

back to his desk. Following the direction of the Sergeant's thumb Kieran found himself in a long corridor. He walked the corridor slowly, checking the tiny lettering on each door. Needless to say, right at the bottom he found the door he was looking for. By the time he had found it, Simon Williams had already been informed of Kieran's arrival.

The lettering read 'SERIOUS CRIME SQUAD'. Kieran smiled and opened the door. The room seemed reasonably well equipped. There were four desks, two computer consoles, and four phones, one on each desk. Two filing cabinets stood with their backs to the wall, on which there was a huge map of Snuggstown. Only one of the desks was occupied. Michael Malone had been in the office since eight o'clock that morning. Although he hadn't been keen to join the Serious Crime Squad in Snuggstown, once Michael applied himself to any task he applied himself one hundred percent. He was sitting at the computer console running the mouse over some files; he looked up and smiled when he saw Kieran.

'Good morning, boss!' Michael played with the word 'boss'.

'Good morning, Michael. So, what do you think of our new office?'

'Oh wonderful, boss, it beats all those plush carpets and smoked-salmon sandwiches we had up in Dublin Castle. And the lads outside, gosh I thought I'd never make it to the office; they had me in stitches laughing. You should see the welcome I got!'

'Yes, I had a fairly chilly reception myself. Anyway, let's get to work. Round up the rest of the squad and we'll have a meeting.'

'I did,' Michael announced with a smile.

'You did what?'

'I got the squad together.'

Kieran looked around the room as if expecting them to pop out of cupboards. 'So, where are they?'

'Well, now that you've arrived, the entire squad is here. We're it!'

'We're the squad! The whole Serious Crime Squad for the whole of Snuggstown?'

'Yes. Great, isn't it?' Michael was not smiling now.

Kieran's face took on a look of bitter disappointment. He paced the room. There was little Michael could do but watch him. Suddenly Kieran stopped. He loosened his tie, opened his top shirt-button, and smiled at Michael.

'Well, Michael, if we're it, then we're it! Let's get the hell out of here and find a coffee shop somewhere so we can talk.'

Fifteen minutes later the two detectives were sitting across the table from each other in the Coffee Hop in Snuggstown village. The place had been called the Coffee Hop for twelve years. When it opened fifteen years ago it was called the Coffee Shop, but three years later the 'S' on the sign outside fell off. By the time the owner got around to thinking about replacing it, the place was known throughout Snuggstown as the Coffee Hop, so he simply left it that way. Kieran stirred his frothy, milky coffee slowly.

'So, did you find out anything this morning?' he asked Michael.

'Everyone I talked to just gave me a frosty reception. Some of them just stared at me as if I had suddenly dropped from outer space. Eventually I dug into their files, they couldn't stop me doing that, and I managed to come across this file here, it's the Serious Crime Squad Active Cases file.' Michael placed a red Twinlock file-cover on the table.

'Well, that's a start,' said Kieran, and he took a bite of his cream cake. Wiping the icing sugar and a little bit of jam from his lips he urged Michael on. 'So tell me, what exactly are they investigating at the moment?'

Michael opened the file. 'Nothing.'

'What do you mean – nothing?'

'Nothing,' Michael repeated, this time slowly, 'as in NOT A THING.'

Kieran stared at Michael with a blank expression on his face. 'Are you telling me there's no serious crime happening in Snuggstown?' Kieran asked Michael as if it were Michael's fault that there was nothing in the file.

'I'm not telling you anything of the sort. I'm telling you that the Active File says that nothing is being investigated. Of course serious crime is happening in Snuggstown. But Simon Williams is the King in Snuggstown. He runs it with an iron fist. He runs the drugs, the protection, the lot. He keeps his head down and his nose clean, and that's that!'

'And who's investigating Simon Williams's activities?'

'Investigate Simple Simon?' Michael began to laugh.

'Wait a minute! Surely if someone is paying protection, someone is out there breaking legs. Or are you telling me that doesn't happen?'

Michael had closed the file now and placed it on the seat beside him. He began to tuck into his own cake. 'There were two murders in Snuggstown last month,' Michael announced with crumbs falling from his mouth.

'So what's happening with those cases?'

'The Serious Crime Squad didn't get them.'

'What?' Kieran was aghast. 'Why not?'

'Well, when I asked, I was told they were drug-related and that the Drug Squad would handle it. There have been no arrests!' Michael said this in a low voice, as if it were a secret.

Kieran covered his face with his hands. The enormity of what he had taken on sank in. After a couple of moments he slowly took his hands away.

'Well, Detective Malone, we'll put a stop to all that! The next serious crime that comes in, drug-related or not, we get it!' Kieran banged his fist on the table as he said this, drawing the attention of the Coffee Hop customers.

Michael leaned across the table and placed his hand on Kieran's arm. 'You know, Kieran, I wasn't looking forward to this job, but now you know what? The bastards in this station are a bit too smug for my liking.'

'Now you're talking, Michael, now you're talking!'

* * *

The McCabe home, Snuggstown, 11.45pm

With Eileen and Mickey already in bed, Sparrow had dozed off on the couch. The ringing of the telephone jarred him awake. It was one of those confused awakenings. At first he couldn't remember where he was. Then he realised he was at home. Next he was wondering what the sound was. Then he realised it was the telephone, but couldn't remember where the telephone was. As he rose from the armchair he discovered his right leg had gone to sleep and he fell down onto one knee. The result of all this was, that by the time he got to the telephone, he was out of breath and Eileen was standing at the top of the stairs. Eileen looked at her watch; it was a quarter to midnight. A telephone call at this hour of the night usually meant family problems. She hoped it wasn't anything to do with her mother. Nervously she listened to Sparrow's half of the conversation.

'Hello? Yeh. I was asleep in the chair. What? But it's nearly midnight. Right. Okay, right. Where? Right, ten minutes. I said all right!' Sparrow hung up and picked up the keys of the car from the telephone table. As he did so he noticed Eileen coming down the stairs. He put his jacket on and smiled at her.

'It's okay, love, go on back to bed.'

But Eileen kept coming. 'Who is it? Who was on the phone?' she asked, concerned.

'It's nothing. It was Teddy. He wants the car!'

Even though she had just done so at the top of the stairs Eileen again looked at her watch. 'At this hour? For what?'

'I don't fuckin' know, love,' Sparrow snapped, then he calmed down. 'Look, I won't be long.' Sparrow had told Eileen of the events in the Falcon Inn on the previous Monday evening. He voiced his concerns that things were getting out of hand. To Eileen's great relief he also, for the first time in six years, told her that he thought he might give up this job. She didn't want to seem too enthusiastic in case he might change his mind just because he thought she was getting her way, the way men can do. So she had simply said, 'Whatever yeh think yourself, love,' but had that night prayed that the idea of giving up his job with Simon Williams would mature in Sparrow's mind. Sparrow hadn't been the same since Tuesday night. He was uneasy – not frightened, but nervy.

Eileen smiled at him and said, 'Go on. And if you get to a garage would yeh get me some milk and bread.'

Sparrow gave her a kiss on the side of the cheek and repeated the order. 'Milk and bread, right! Go on back to bed, love, see yeh!'

Although Sparrow had told Teddy that he would be there in ten minutes it was actually twenty minutes before he arrived at the statue of the Madonna outside the Legion of Mary Hall, where the Morgan brothers were waiting. As usual, Teddy climbed into the front. Bubbles was moaning even as he climbed into the back.

'I'm fuckin' freezin',' he groaned.

'You took your fuckin' time,' Teddy said aggressively.

Unfazed, Sparrow wiped his sleepy eyes. 'Yeh well, I had to go to a garage. So, what's up?'

'Nothin's up. Just drive!' Teddy ordered.

'Yeh, just drive!' Bubbles repeated.

'Drive to where?' Sparrow asked, trying to sound as patronising as he could.

'Magpie Grove,' Teddy barked.

'Yeh, Magpie Grove,' Bubbles repeated.

'Magpie? Yeh could have bleedin' walked there!' Sparrow declared as he noisily let the handbrake off and pushed the lever into drive.

'Just fuckin' drive, will yeh?' Teddy barked again.

'Yeh! Fuckin' drive,' came from the back.

Somebody in Dublin Corporation must have invested great ingenuity into naming all the streets in one part of Snuggstown after birds. There was Flamingo Road, Toucan

Hill, Emu Grove and other very exotic names; however, there was no Sparrow nor Crow! In fact, Magpie Grove was the only street named after any bird that might be found in Ireland. These were the ways of the Corporation's Planning Department. Within minutes the Jag was turning into the south end of Magpie Grove. Eighty percent of the residents in this street were unemployed. This left little money to be invested in their gardens. Still, they kept them as good as they could and most of them were not bad at all.

'Take it slowly now!' Teddy instructed as they drove down the street.

'What are yeh lookin' for?' Sparrow asked.

'Easy, go on. Easy!' Teddy was engrossed in his task of trying to see door numbers in the dark.

'I said, what are yeh lookin' for?' Sparrow asked again, as he knew a lot of people on Magpie Grove.

'Just keep going,' Teddy snapped and began counting out loud. 'Twenty-two, twenty-four, twenty-six – hold it!'

Sparrow stopped the car. 'So now what?' he asked, but the question had barely left his lips when his indifferent manner changed to one of shock.

'All right, Teddy, all clear,' Bubbles called, looking out the back window.

'Right, Bubbles, let's get to work.' Teddy pulled something woollen from his inside pocket. It was a balaclava. He pulled it over his face and began to climb out of the car.

'What the fuck? Twenty-eight? That's young PJ Duff's place. Wait a minute!' The plot dawned on Sparrow, and he grabbed Teddy's sleeve. Teddy sat back into the car and looked at Sparrow. In the balaclava his face was terrifying.

'You keep this car runnin', d'yeh hear me?' Teddy

ordered, jabbing a finger into Sparrow's shoulder.

Sparrow tried to argue with him. 'But wait a minute, Teddy, he has a wife and a young kid, for fuck's sake.'

Teddy was out of the car now. Sparrow called after him, pleading, 'He was only doin' his job, for Christ's sake!'

Teddy put his head back into the doorway of the car. 'Yeh, and I'm only doin' mine, and if you know what's good for yeh, you'll shut the fuck up and do yours.'

Sparrow had gone pale and his mouth was dry. When he spoke it felt like his tongue was stuck to the roof of his mouth. He shook his dazed head. 'This is nothing to do with me. I'm not a getaway driver!' Sparrow was starting to rant and his breath was coming in short bursts now. By this time Bubbles had joined Teddy at the side of the car.

Teddy leaned into the car again. 'You're whatever Mr Williams says you are. Now shut up, yeh whingin' bastard.' Teddy left the car and his form was replaced by Bubbles.

'Yeh, bastard, and whingin' too!'

The two men opened the gate of number twenty-eight. They strolled up the path like they were out for a casual walk. Sparrow began to bang the steering wheel with the palms of his hands.

'Fuck! He's only a kid. Fuck, fuck, fuck!' He was beginning to crack.

***

Herbert Park Hotel, Ballsbridge, 12.40am

'This is great, Kieran,' Moya exclaimed as she glanced around the luscious surroundings. She was right. The

Herbert Park Hotel in Dublin is one of the plushest and most luxurious. The restaurant, where Kieran and Moya were sitting now, was renowned for its food and wonderful service.

Moya continued. 'I mean, when you said let's go out for a midnight supper, I thought you were talking about something simple, I didn't think you meant this.' She hadn't been expecting a treat like this tonight. Kieran smiled, enjoying Moya's excitement and beginning to buzz himself with the sense of occasion. 'Well, I started in my new promotion today and I kind of felt a bit special, so I wanted you to feel special too.'

Moya stretched her arm across the table and squeezed Kieran's hand. 'It's beautiful.' She smiled at him. The waiter arrived with two Caesar salads and placed them in front of the pair. Kieran raised his glass of wine, Moya raised hers, and they clinked.

'To us,' said Kieran.

Moya smiled and repeated the toast.

Like young lovers they sipped their wine while maintaining eye contact. Moya began to eat her salad and Kieran followed. He had his fork halfway to his lips when his bleeper sounded. He froze, his eyes locked onto his wife's.

'You'd better ring in,' Moya said flatly.

Kieran shrugged apologetically and left the table. Moya looked after him as he walked toward the reception desk.

'It has begun!' she whispered softly to herself and the magic died.

Kieran walked past the reception desk and around to the line of telephone booths on the landing of the stairs that led down to the car park. They were all in use. His heart was thumping. This was his first bleep. He went back to Reception and spoke to a pretty girl behind the desk.

'Excuse me, could I use the house phone?' Expecting a protest and directions to the telephone booths, Kieran was now rummaging in his inside pocket for his police identification. He needn't have bothered.

'Certainly!' The receptionist smiled and placed the telephone in front of Kieran. He tapped out his office number and waited. He looked over at Moya; she was looking at him. He waved and smiled. She returned his wave but not his smile.

When the telephone was answered at the other end Kieran simply said, 'Clancy.' He listened to Michael Malone, amazed at what he was hearing.

'Magpie Grove? How long ago? It certainly does! I'll be there in fifteen minutes.' He replaced the handset in the cradle and smiled at the receptionist. He was dreading the thought of telling Moya he had to go. He turned to find her standing beside him wearing her coat. Dangling from her outstretched index finger were the car keys.

'Off you go. You take the car, I'll get a taxi. I paid the bill for the wine and the salads.'

Kieran took the keys from her finger and kissed her on the cheek. He held her in his arms and whispered into her ear, 'You're special. Do you know that? You're really special!' And he was gone.

Moya stood in the lobby looking after him. As he left the hotel she once again spoke to herself. 'That's the problem, Kieran, you see I'm not special.'

'I beg your pardon, Madam?' the receptionist said.

'Can you call me a taxi, please?' Moya asked.

Downtown, Dublin City, 6.00am

Sparrow McCabe was running harder and longer than he had ever run in his life. He had been running now for over five hours. He had no idea where he was running to, and what he was running from was just too confusing, too horrific even to think about. Life as he knew it had come to an end. He had to stop, he had to take a rest. His heart was pounding so hard it sounded like drums in his ears. His muscles were not getting enough oxygen and his strength began to slow.

He stopped at an electrical shop with a recessed doorway and leaned back in against the door. Slowly he slid to a sitting position. He put his arms around his legs and pulled his knees up tightly into his chest. He sank his head to his knees. Like an ostrich putting his head in the sand he hoped when he looked up it would all be gone. It wasn't. The scene went through his mind again.

The Morgan brothers had knocked on the door of number twenty-eight. They were excited. It took two further rattles on the door-knocker before there was any sign of life inside the house. They could hear somebody stumbling down the stairs. A light went on in the inner hallway and through the frosted glass they could make out the shape of a young woman. As soon as she had opened it a crack, Bubbles kicked the door fully open and covered her mouth to stifle her scream while he pushed her inside. Immediately PJ Duff came stumbling down the stairs. Instinctively he threw himself at Bubbles, disturbing Bubbles enough to release his hand slightly from the woman's mouth. She let out half a scream but was stopped by a punch from Teddy. Upstairs a baby cried. In a rage PJ now turned his attention to Teddy. He was untrained and, having just woken, was disorientated, and before he could even get a hand on Teddy, Teddy's pistol whipped him on the side of the head. PJ crumpled to the hall floor.

Grabbing PJ by the scruff of the neck, Teddy dragged him out of the hall and into the Duffs' small front room. Bubbles followed the two with one hand over the woman's mouth, dragging her by the hair. The woman put up a mighty struggle and even under Bubbles's hand her screams were audible. By the time Bubbles got the woman into the front room Teddy already had PJ sitting in an upright chair. PJ was dazed but conscious. The flaying of the woman's arms and legs, banging off tables and the door, was making a racket. Teddy kicked her in the stomach and she immediately quietened. Bubbles lifted her roughly into a lying position on the couch. From under his coat he produced a baton and pinned the woman across the throat on the couch. The woman was in pain and terrified. She looked up into Teddy's balaclava-clad eyes.

'My baby. Please let me go to my baby!' she begged.

'Shut up! Just stay quiet and yeh'll go to yer baby soon enough,' Bubbles advised her, but the woman was too terrified to understand what he was talking about.

Sparrow had been watching all this from the car. He saw PJ stumbling on the stairs. He saw PJ throw himself at Bubbles. He watched as the woman got the punch from Teddy. And he saw the helplessness of the couple as they were dragged like sacks of coal through their own home. He was gripped with anguish.

Don't get involved, Sparrow! he told himself. Don't get involved. He was still banging the steering wheel, fighting back the tears. From an upstairs window he heard a baby cry. That was enough.

'Ah fuck it,' he exclaimed as he opened the door of the car. Sparrow jumped out and ran to the front door. The baby's cries were now piercing his ears. Sparrow could hear PJ's wife from the front room begging Bubbles to let her go to her baby. He burst into the room. Bubbles still had the young woman pinned to the couch with a baton. She was bleeding from a cut above her eye and through her nose. All the time she was pleading with Bubbles.

'My baby, my baby!' PJ was sitting upright, covered in blood, so much so that it was difficult to tell where the blood was coming from.

'Stop it! That's enough!' Sparrow screamed as he tried to drag Teddy away.

Teddy was startled by Sparrow's arrival. 'What the fuck are you doin'? Get out to the car, yeh fuckin' shithead.' He shook Sparrow off and turned his attention again to PJ.

PJ was just mumbling on and on. 'I needed the job ... I couldn't do anything ... The baby, let her go to the baby. Take me away. The baby!'

'For Christ's sake!' Sparrow screamed.

Teddy reached into his coat and pulled out a pistol. 'Shut the fuck up you,' he screamed at Sparrow. The pistol made a 'crack' sound. PJ's head jerked back and then his body slumped forward onto the floor in a heap.

'My baby!' The woman screeched again. Bubbles jumped up, slapped her face and ran out the door. Teddy pocketed the pistol and turned to leave.

Sparrow stood transfixed, aghast at the scene and overwhelmed by what had happened.

Teddy returned and dragged him away by the collar. 'Move, yeh fuckin' dope, move!' The two brothers ran to the car, Teddy dragging Sparrow. Behind him, Sparrow heard the baby's cries which were now fretful. Bubbles dived into the back of the car. Teddy pushed Sparrow around to the driver's side and ran back to the passenger side.

Sparrow stared at the driver's door. 'No. No! Fuck this – no! Not for me.' Sparrow began to walk dizzily away from the car, mumbling.

'Sparrow, yeh yellow bastard! Get back and drive this car. Sparrow!' Teddy called angrily.

'What's wrong?' Bubbles called from the back seat.

'It's Sparrow, he's lost it, his bottle's gone – again!'

'What bottle, his bottle of what?' Bubbles was now totally confused.

'Bubbles, shut the fuck up, will yeh? Sparrow!' Teddy shouted again. Sparrow didn't move.

'Ah fuck yeh!' Teddy roared. He ran around the car and got into the driver's seat himself. The car sped off. As it rounded the bend at the end of Magpie Grove a pint of milk flew out the window and smashed against the kerb.

***

Sparrow was squeezing his legs so much now that they started to get pins and needles. He was sobbing out loud and uncontrollably. There was a display of television sets inside the window of the electrical shop. As a news programme

103

came on, Sparrow slowly stood up. He looked at the televisions and they all showed the same picture. There was no sound, but Sparrow didn't need any sound for he knew the whole story. The pictures haunted him. On screen the news reporter was standing in front of the Duff home. There were police cars all over the place in the background. He saw PJ's shocked wife being led to an ambulance. The reporter moved to a policeman for comment, and the man waved him away.

There were a number of other televisions in the shop. Suddenly the screens all changed and Sparrow fell back against the wall. On one screen Sparrow saw the fight, his fight in Madrid with the Spaniard. On another the Morgan brothers were staring into the camera, pointing with an index finger at Sparrow. They began to laugh. On another screen Simple Simon and Angie were laughing. On another the blood-covered face of the Spaniard was laughing.

Sparrow screamed and began to run again. Dawn was breaking and the sun was rising in the east. In his confused madness, Sparrow made the decision to run toward the sun. Not just in its direction – but actually all the way to it.

* * *

The McCabe home, 6.40am

It was difficult for Michael Malone to get parking for his car outside the McCabe home, as there were already three squad cars parked there. Kieran had a puzzled look on his face as he hurried from the car to the front door, which was under guard by a young uniformed officer. Kieran flashed his ID.

'What are you doing here?' he asked the young lad.

'We're here on a search, Sergeant, on foot of a warrant,' the officer answered officiously.

Kieran replaced his ID in his hip pocket. When he gave his next order to the officer, it was not in an angry tone, but it had enough edge in it for the young man to know that it was not to be questioned.

'I want this search stopped now. Assemble all the men in the front garden, here, now!'

The officer spun around and made his way quickly upstairs. Kieran was joined at the front door by Michael, and together they stepped into Sparrow's home.

As Kieran entered the front room he had his first glimpse of Eileen McCabe. She was standing by the fireplace. In the fire grate the ash and wasted cinders gave the room a stark feel. Eileen was standing, one hand on the mantelpiece, her other arm wrapped around her son Mickey, who was holding her so tight he seemed welded to her. They were both terrified. Eileen held her cigarette in her hand, which was shaking so much that she might have been holding a pneumatic drill. Kieran was struck by how pretty she was. For some inexplicable reason he had expected her to be a short, dumpy woman. There was no doubting who was the father of the young boy. He was the spitting image of Sparrow from head to toe.

Eileen looked up at Kieran. 'Join the party,' she said.

Kieran glanced around the room. Cushions had been ripped open. The contents of shelves tipped onto the floor. Armchairs upturned. He felt embarrassed.

'I'm Detective Sergeant Kieran Clancy, head of the Serious Crime Squad at Snuggstown,' Kieran said as he offered his hand.

'Yeh right,' was all Eileen replied. She didn't attempt to shake Kieran's hand.

'I'm sorry about all this. It was uncalled for and unnecessary. I've called a halt to it. I'll leave two officers with you to help you put things back the way they were.'

'I don't want you to leave anybody here, just get these people out of my house,' Eileen snapped.

Kieran bent over, righted an armchair and sat down. 'Have you heard from Sparrow?' he asked.

'No,' Eileen replied. She didn't look at Kieran, but the boy, Mickey, was staring at him. Kieran smiled at him and the boy turned his face into his mother's body.

'The woman – Mrs Duff – she knows Sparrow well –' Kieran began.

'She's mistaken,' Eileen snapped.

Now Kieran lit a cigarette. 'No, she's not. And you know she's not, Mrs McCabe!'

'Do I now? How the fuck would you know what I'd know?' Eileen looked into Kieran's eyes for the first time.

'Look, Mrs McCabe, if I have to I'll take you down to the station.' As Kieran said this Mickey pulled away from his mother.

'Yeh can't do that,' he shouted. 'Unless you want to arrest her first. That's the law, pal!' He had spunk.

Eileen stepped toward him and put her hands on his shoulders. 'Quiet, Mickey. Go out to the kitchen and make us another cup of tea, love, will yeh? Go on now, like a good man.' Eileen's tone was soft as she pushed him towards the door.

'Okay Ma, but tell him to fuck off!'

Instinctively Eileen clipped him on the ear. 'You mind

your tongue, yeh little bastard!' she snapped.

Kieran was smiling as he looked after the boy leaving the room. 'He seems like a good kid,' he commented.

'He is,' was all Eileen said.

Kieran stood up. 'Look, Mrs McCabe,' he said calmly, 'where would he usually go?'

Eileen smiled at the policeman. 'You mean like after he fuckin' shoots someone? Now, let me see! It's either golf or tennis – what day is it?'

Kieran smiled at her – he had deserved that and he knew it. Suddenly the phone rang loudly. Both Eileen and Kieran snapped a look at it immediately. Kieran then looked back to Eileen. Her face was anguished.

'Answer it,' Kieran said with a wave of his hand towards the phone.

'No, you answer it.' Eileen looked away and took a drag of her cigarette.

'If I answer it he'll hang up,' Kieran said.

The phone went on ringing. Eileen looked directly at Kieran. 'If it's him,' she said.

'Answer it, Mrs McCabe. I won't interfere, I promise. At least you'll know he's safe. You can tell him I'm here, and if he wants to talk to me I'll listen.'

Slowly Eileen moved away from the fireplace to the phone. She picked it up.

'*Eileen? It's me, love!*' Sparrow sounded terrified.

'Yeh, I know,' Eileen said, and glanced sideways at the policeman.

'*They killed Duff, Eileen. PJ, PJ Duff, they fuckin' killed him. I ran off. The bastards, they just walked in and killed him.*' Sparrow was frantic.

107

Eileen was beginning to get upset. 'Sparrow, the police are here.'

'Pretend you're talkin' to your mother.'

'They know who I'm talkin' to, Sparrow. There's a detective here ...'

'Clancy, Kieran Clancy.' Kieran took a step towards the phone as he gave Eileen his name.

'Kieran Clancy. He says he'll listen to yeh – whatever that means.'

'I didn't kill him, Eileen.'

'I know. But – ah here, Sparrow, talk to him.' Eileen held the phone towards Clancy. Clancy took the receiver and asked, 'Are you all right?'

'Why? Are you doin' a fuckin' survey? Of course I'm not all right! What are you doin' there? In my house? The woman knows – Mrs Duff – she'll tell yeh. I shot no-one. Is Mickey all right? Ah Jesus!'

'Calm down, Sparrow. Mickey's fine. Your wife is fine. Look, we know you didn't kill Duff. But you were there. We need to know why you were there, and who the two men with you were.'

'Will yeh fuck off! Do you think I'm a nutcase? Me life wouldn't be worth a shit if I told you anythin'. Forget it. No way!' Sparrow was still wildly agitated.

'Listen to sense, Sparrow. We're going to get you one way or another.'

Kieran tried to reason with the man, but there was no reasoning with Sparrow, not in his state of mind.

'I can't ... it's ... it's – no way.'

There was a tiny click and the phone went dead. Kieran held the receiver limp in his hand and looked at Eileen.

'He's gone,' he said simply.

Eileen exhaled a long puff of smoke as she stared into space. 'What's new? He's been gone years now.'

Kieran replaced the receiver in its cradle. The young policeman that Kieran had met guarding the door came into the room and announced that all the officers involved in the search had now assembled in the garden. Kieran went out to speak to them. There were six of them. Kieran recognised one or two faces from Snuggstown station.

'Who led this search?' Kieran asked.

A young, lean, pale-faced guard stepped forward. 'I did, Sergeant.'

'On whose authority?' Kieran asked him.

The young guard produced a search warrant from his pocket and handed it to Kieran. 'I was given this by Sergeant Muldoon,' he stated. At the mention of Muldoon's name, Kieran looked over at Michael. Michael simply threw his eyes to heaven. Kieran handed back the search warrant.

'Gentlemen, this is my operation. Sergeant Muldoon had no authority to send you here. You can return to your posts. I'll talk to Sergeant Muldoon when I get back.'

Somewhat disgruntled, the group of guards left and Kieran went back into the house. He met Mickey in the hall, carefully carrying a mug of hot tea in to his mother.

'Can you manage that?' Kieran asked the boy. Mickey didn't even look up, but walked straight past Kieran into the room.

'Tough kid, eh?' Michael said. Kieran nodded. 'God love him, he must be terrified,' Michael added. They followed the child into the room.

Eileen was sipping her mug of tea and once again the

boy was welded to her side.

'Did you mean that?' Eileen asked Kieran.

'Sorry?'

'Did you mean that, what you said to Sparrow on the phone? That you know he didn't kill PJ Duff – do you mean that?' Eileen desperately wanted confirmation from the detective that her husband was not a murderer.

'Yes, Mrs McCabe, I meant it. Your husband is not a murderer. But he knows who is, and so I have to find him, I have to help him tell the truth.'

While she was taking this in, Eileen gently and slowly rubbed her hand up and down young Mickey's back. She was beginning to relax.

'I may need to talk to you again sometime today, Mrs McCabe. Will you be in?' Kieran asked.

'No, not here, I'm takin' Mickey to me mother's. We'll stay there for a while. It'll be safer there.'

Kieran nodded and went over to the window. He looked out into the early morning. 'I wonder where Sparrow will stay – that's safe?'

CHAPTER TEN

Monday, 16 December
Offices of Williams Wholesale Depot, 3pm

NOBODY WAS QUITE SURE exactly what Williams Wholesale Depot actually wholesaled. Whatever it was, it obviously made big profits, for Simon Williams's office in the building was huge and had all the trappings of financial success.

Simon's steel-tipped heels clicked on the cobble-block maple floor now as he paced the room. Bubbles and Teddy simply stood in the same position they'd been in since they walked into the office half an hour ago, as if they were playing a game of statues. For minutes on end Simon continued to pace and the Morgan brothers never took their eyes off him. Simon walked to the panoramic window that overlooked the docks. He stopped, his legs apart. He clasped his hands behind his back, stood for a couple of moments like a king overseeing his realm, then slowly turned and returned to his desk. When his fist slammed onto his desk all of the items on it – the telephone, his writing pad, his diary, and sundry little office items – leaped into the air simultaneously. Strangely enough, both Morgan brothers also left the ground.

'Don't give me that shit!' Simon screamed. 'I want that little bastard. It's been four days and not so much as a fuckin' whisper.' He was in a total fury. He stood up again and pointed out the window.

'Somebody out there knows where he is!' He pointed silently at Teddy. Teddy was unsure whether or not this statement required an answer, but he decided to venture some kind of explanation.

'Nobody's talkin', Mr Williams. Sparrow has a lot of friends out there.'

This was a mistake. Simon walked over to Teddy. 'Nobody's talkin'? What do you mean, nobody's talkin'? What are you runnin' out there – a debatin' society? Make the fuckers talk! Simple! Spill some blood! Then they'll talk! They'll fuckin' sing!' The telephone on Simon's desk beeped and began to flash a little red light. Simon pushed the button and yelled into the intercom. 'What!'

'There's a Detective Sergeant Clancy to see you,' a nervous voice replied.

Simon was startled at first, but then began to gather himself. He straightened his tie and brushed down his jacket. 'Oh! Yeh. Right. Eh, give me a minute, and then send him in.'

'That's the new fella from Serious Crimes. Do you want us to stay, Mr Williams?' Teddy asked.

Simon walked around his desk straight to Teddy, their noses nearly touching. 'No. I do not want you to stay, Teddy, I want you to go. Go and catch me a Sparrow. And if he won't come out, then fuckin' flush him out.' He pinched Teddy's cheek and said, 'Tweet, Tweet!'

Bubbles began to giggle. 'Nice one, Mr Williams, tweet, tweet.' When Simon turned around, Teddy kicked Bubbles on the shin.

The Morgan brothers left through a side door and moments later Kieran Clancy entered the room through the main door. He looked calm and cool. Simon came around the desk with an outstretched hand.

'Detective Clancy, come in and make yourself comfortable,' he said, welcoming him grandly.

Kieran took Simon's hand and surprised Simon with the warmth of his shake. 'Thanks very much, Mr Williams, it's very good of you to see me without an appointment.' Kieran smiled. Simon ushered him to a chair and indicated that he should sit down. He waved away Kieran's thank you.

'No appointment is necessary for a member of the force, Detective Clancy. I like to think we can help each other. I'm a great supporter of the local police.' Simon was every inch the local businessman.

'I heard that, all right. Some of the lads are very fond of you.' Kieran took out a cigarette and held it up as if to ask if it was okay to smoke. With a wave of his hand Simon indicated his assent.

'Well, Detective Clancy,' Simon responded, 'I like to think that the members of the force can come to me in times of ... of personal emergency. And they do.'

'Ah, that's nice. Now, as the new head of the Serious Crime Squad, Mr Williams, I thought I'd better introduce myself to you on a one-to-one basis, so to speak.'

Simon smiled a knowing smile and nodded. 'I can appreciate that, Detective. A private chat, so to speak.'

Kieran lit up a cigarette and took a drag. 'Exactly.' He blew out a puff of smoke. 'You see, Mr Williams, I don't know what kind of arrangement you had with my predecessor, and that's his business, but I thought I'd come over and make my own deal with you. Are you with me?'

'All the way – eh, may I call you Kieran?'

'Eh – no,' Kieran said, and carried on, 'so, here's the new deal, Mr Williams. You stop committing crimes on the street and I won't arrest you.'

Simon stared at the young detective dumbfounded.

'So, what do you think? Are we on?'

Simon Williams gathered himself, and seeing that he had been taken in, leaned back in his chair, took out a cigar, lit it and exhaled a long plume of blue smoke. He smiled at Kieran.

'Now, aren't you the smart arse!' he said. The bitterness in his voice was not missed by Kieran.

Kieran poked the two fingers that were holding his cigarette in Simon's direction. 'You can count on it, Mr Williams!' He smiled and took another drag from his cigarette. At no time did his blue eyes leave Simon Williams's.

Simon leaned forward in his chair and placed both elbows on the desk. 'And you, my detective friend, can count on this. If you come into my patch like fuckin' Rambo, it will be a short stay.'

Kieran stood up and leaned on the desk with one hand. With the other hand he stubbed out his cigarette on the leather inlay in the centre of Simon's desk. He looked into Simon's face.

'First of all, Mr Williams, I'm not your friend. Secondly,

this is my patch. Thirdly, I'm not Rambo. And, Mr Willliams, your time is up!' He turned his back on Williams and began to walk towards the door, brushing his jacket off. At the door he turned and pointed directly at Simon.

'Now, Mr Williams, I'm off to find Sparrow McCabe – to sort of get things rolling.'

'Now you're talking, Detective,' Simon sneered. 'That's what you should be doing instead of threatening local businessmen. You should be off catching that murderer.'

Kieran looked at Williams with a smile on his face. 'Oh, he's not my murderer, Mr Williams, he's my witness. After I get him, then I'll come and get you. Simple!'

Simon stood at his desk and spoke through his teeth. 'I'll have you writing parking tickets in a month's time.'

Kieran turned to deliver his parting shot. 'I beat you to it, Mr Williams. Go and check your Jaguar! Good luck.' He left and closed the door firmly behind him.

For a few moments Simon stared at the closed door, his lip quivering with anger. He stubbed out his cigar in the ashtray and he went to the window. He stood, legs apart, hands clasped behind his back. He was thinking.

***

Across the street a shadowy figure stepped from the darkness. It was Sparrow McCabe. He had a frown on his face as he watched Detective Clancy's car drive away. He began to walk down Dock Street towards the city centre, his brain trying to figure out what exactly could have been going on between those two. He wondered about Clancy's chuckle as he passed the Jaguar. At the bottom of Dock Street he turned into Misery Hill, where there was a lit phone-box. Sparrow took a handkerchief from his pocket and wrapped it around his hand. He glanced around to see he was alone, stepped into the phone-box and smashed the light. In the darkness he inserted a coin in the box and punched in his mother-in-law's number. He waited for an answer. Sparrow was relieved when Eileen answered.

'Hello, Eileen love. It's me. I'm fine. Listen, I'm gonna get somebody to call up to our place tomorrow. I want you to get some things together for me.'

* * *

The Clancy home, 8pm

The room was festooned with Christmas decorations. Claire and Mary were playing on the floor. They had five dolls and were making five separate beds from little bits of blankets and cushions that they had taken off the couch. The scent of freshly-bathed children filled the room. From the kitchen came the sound of pots banging and plates being laid out. Moya was busy preparing for the Christmas dinner-party that night for her parents.

Kieran sat in the armchair by the fire, fondly watching his daughters play Mother. Slowly his eyes drifted up to the Christmas tree. The tiny Christmas lights twinkled and reflected in the silvery tinsel. Tiny angels perched on the end of each branch. At the tip of the tree stood one large white angel dressed in white, with her arms outstretched.

'Good will to all men,' Kieran read – except husbands, was his next thought. In the ten days since the PJ Duff murder case had started, Kieran had slept with his wife only three times. He was getting what he called the 'do not adjust your set' treatment – all picture, no sound.

His daughters were less affected with his absence, for he would get home in the evenings and have a couple of hours with them before they went to bed. Unfortunately criminals do not work nine-to-five. Most of Kieran's investigations took place at night and into the early hours of the morning. This was not appreciated by Moya. One would imagine that the daughter of a policeman would be well prepared for a time when she became the wife of a policeman herself. This was not the case. Moya hated her childhood memories of her father never being there. Now it seemed her childhood was coming back to haunt her and she was not amused.

The doorbell chimed and from the kitchen Moya called out to Kieran. 'That'll be them, Kieran.'

Kieran rose to get the door, on the way informing the children, 'Granddad and Grandma are here.'

The children shrieked with delight and ran to get to the door before their father. Ned and Carmel Connolly had beaming, festive smiles on their faces. The children virtually attacked them.

'Easy, easy, let's get our coats off first,' Ned said to his grandchildren. Kieran took the coats and hung them in the hall as kisses were exchanged by grandchildren and grandparents. Kieran opened his arms to embrace Carmel. 'Merry Christmas, Carmel, it's great to see you.'

'Where's my daughter?' Carmel asked looking around the room.

'In the kitchen, as usual, cooking up a storm. I think you're getting a steak with diane sauce – and I'm going to get poisoned!' Kieran raised his eyes to heaven.

Carmel chuckled. 'Oh I see, we're at that stage, are we? Well, I'll just go in and give her a hand.' And Carmel headed for the kitchen.

The children had now calmed down and had gone back to playing with their dolls. The two men strolled into the sitting room.

'Will you have a drink, Ned?'

'I will, Kieran, and as I'm staying the night make it a hardy one! I haven't been able to have a decent drink over the last week with these bloody drink driving checkpoints! Damned Gardaí!' The two men laughed. Kieran poured two stiff drinks and handed one to Ned.

The Commissioner eyed his son-in-law. 'Well, I hear you settled into the Serious Crime Squad out in Snuggstown pretty quickly?' Ned walked to the couch, settled himself and stretched out his legs.

Kieran saw that his father-in-law was getting comfortable. 'Kick off your shoes there, Ned.'

'I will if you don't mind, Kieran.' It was a habit with policemen: the only true way to real comfort was to kick off the shoes and walk barefoot on a carpet – it probably came from spending a lot of time on the beat.

Kieran settled himself in the armchair. 'What d'you mean, Ned? What have you heard?' Kieran asked.

'I heard about your visit up to Mr Williams's office,' the Commissioner said with a knowing smile.

'News travels fast,' Kieran chuckled.

'Well, tread carefully there, son. I don't want you

upsetting the apple-cart.'

Kieran frowned at his father-in-law. 'Upsetting what apple-cart? Simon Williams is the root cause of ninety percent of the problems in Snuggstown. If I can rattle him in any way, I will, and I don't see it as upsetting any apple-cart. Exactly whose apple-cart are we talking about here?'

'Everybody has their suspicions about Williams,' the Commissioner said, 'but nothing has been proved in a court room. I just don't want you going in there gung-ho and thinking you can rattle this fellow easily. He's a cool customer, Kieran.'

'He's an extortionist, he's a drug-pusher, he's a scumbag and a murderer, and I intend to nail him for this latest murder.' Kieran spat this out, but was glad to note that at each punctuation his father-in-law was nodding.

'Well, unofficially keep me informed of what's going on, and officially if there's anything I can do you just call.' Ned raised his glass.

'Well, from what you've said I hardly think you need me to keep you informed. But I appreciate the offer. Tell me, Ned, what d'you know about a Sergeant Muldoon?'

'That creature?' Ned quickly retorted. 'He was suspended about five years ago for conduct unbecoming of an officer. He'd been sent to arrest some young fellow and he beat him within an inch of his life. The rumour at the time was that the arrest was just a bogus thing, and that really Muldoon was doing a bit of enforcing for Williams, but nothing was ever proven. He's kept his head down since though. Is he giving you a hard time?'

'Yes, he is. But I don't mind that, I can take a hard time. I'm just wondering if he's on Williams's payroll. I don't want him messing up my investigation.'

'Do you want him taken out?'

'No, not yet.'

'Well, just let me know when. I can have him out of there on the pretext of special training at a moment's notice.' There was no sound coming from the kitchen now. Ned nodded towards the kitchen door. 'How's the new life going down with Moya?'

'Badly, to put it mildly,' Kieran said.

'Oh then, she's her mother's daughter!' Ned raised his glass again in a silent toast.

***

When the welcoming hugs had been exchanged in the kitchen by mother and daughter, Moya went back to work. While she worked she spent fifteen minutes bemoaning her husband's new promotion. Carmel listened dutifully and made no comment, letting her daughter go on and on. When Moya had spilled out all her grievances, she looked to her mother for comment. She was surprised at what she got.

'Well, dear, if that's the case then the only thing you can do is leave him!'

Moya wasn't just surprised, she was stunned. Carmel adored Kieran. Carmel was of the opinion that Kieran was the best thing that had ever happened to Moya. Moya stared dumbfounded at her mother. Carmel took in her daughter's questioning gaze and began to explain.

'That's all you can do, Moya. You have two options:

120

either you stay and support your husband or you leave.' Carmel leaned over the salad bowl and plucked out a scallion. She dipped it in some mayonnaise and took a bite. Chewing it, she smiled at her daughter. 'I love scallions!'

'That's not fair, Mum,' Moya said.

'No, it's not fair, dear. But life isn't fair, Moya. I stayed with your father because I love him, not because I loved his job. I hate his job, I have always hated his job, but I loved him. I had an option too – I could have left him. But then I wouldn't have him at all! So I made a decision: to have him for five minutes in a day was better for me than to not have him at all. So I didn't try to compete with his job. I just tried to live my own life and love him in the moments we had together. I know many women who aren't married to policemen and have their husbands home at half-past six every day, and they just sit watching television – they don't talk, they don't do things together, in fact they don't even have each other for five minutes. They're just bored. Kieran will work the most unreasonable, unenviable hours possible, doing a task that is thankless ninety percent of the time. But Moya, when he's with you, he will be with you.'

Moya began to sob. Carmel took her daughter in her arms, laid her head on her shoulder and brushed her fingers through her daughter's hair, just like she had done when Moya was ten years old.

'Help me, Mum, please! It's so hard.'

'I will dear, don't you worry. I will!'

Ned and Kieran were discussing the prospects for World Cup qualification by the Irish soccer team when the two women re-entered the room. Moya went to the table to make the final adjustments. Carmel sat beside her husband.

Kieran poured Carmel a glass of wine, then sat down again to wait. When she decided that the table was ready for dinner, Moya went directly to Kieran's chair. In front of her parents she bent and kissed him softly on the lips.

Then she straightened up and announced, 'Dinner is served, everybody.'

A little stunned, Kieran glanced over at Carmel. Carmel smiled and winked.

* * *

St Thomas's Boxing Club, 10.30pm

The outside of the boxing club looked dull. Christmas lights had been threaded around the edge of the sign that read St Thomas's Boxing Club, but it did little to alleviate the dour look. The sign was lit by a single, cheap spot-lamp. Sparrow had been standing in a doorway across the street for two hours now. Nobody had left the club for over thirty minutes, and he was sure that the club was now empty, except of course for Froggy. He felt fairly sure it was safe to make his move.

With the main lights off and just four single bulbs hung around the hall, the inside of the club looked gloomy. It was quiet except for the slap, slap and squeak of the punch bag that Froggy was attempting to box. Froggy stopped boxing for a moment and cocked his ear as he thought he heard the door open and close. There was no further sound so he went back to his bag. Froggy then heard footsteps on the wooden floor. He was not frightened, he didn't know how to be frightened. So he called out, 'Hawoo? The club is over now. Bye, bye!'

Out of the darkness Froggy heard a voice he recognised,

it was Sparrow. 'It's okay. It's only me, Froggy!'

Froggy's face lit up. As Sparrow stepped into the light Froggy ran over and hugged him. Then Froggy took up a boxing stance. 'Spawoo! Box, Spawoo. Come on, I box yeh.' Froggy began to get excited.

Sparrow put his hands over Froggy's gloves. 'Not now, Froggy, we box later!'

'Later. In the minute. I box yeh. Knock your fuckin' block off!'

'Yeh, Froggy, in a minute. I want to ask you some questions first.' Sparrow took Froggy and walked him to the edge of the room where he sat on a bench. The illumination from the street turned both their faces pale blue. Sparrow put his hand up to Froggy's chin and turned Froggy to face him. He looked into Froggy's eyes.

'Now I want you to listen carefully, Froggy, and think for me, okay?'

Froggy nodded. 'I'm thinkin'. Ooooh I'm thinkin'.'

'Wait till I ask a question first, then think. Was there anybody askin' about me here? Now think.'

Froggy turned his face away from Sparrow. He leaned over and put his head in his hands. He began to moan and groan, and then suddenly lifted up his head.

Sparrow's eyes widened. 'What? What is it, Froggy?'

Froggy smiled at him. 'I'm finished thinkin'.'

'And? Was there?'

'No. Box now, Spawoo.' Froggy stood up. 'Fuckin' kill yeh, knock yer fuckin' head off. Box yeh. Box yeh.'

Sparrow stood up, a little frustrated, and pushed Froggy back down onto the bench. 'No, Froggy, no boxin'. I want yeh to do me a favour.'

Froggy's face grew sad. 'Only messin', Spawoo, won't box your head off. Just box yeh, come on.' Froggy had his arms outstretched. Sparrow pushed Froggy's arms down and put an arm around him.

'This is important, Froggy. I'm in big trouble. There are some people after me.' Sparrow spoke very gravely.

'Will I box them for yeh, Sparrow? I'll knock their fuckin' blocks off, I box them.'

Sparrow smiled, relaxed and hugged the man. 'I know yeh would, Froggy, but not this time. Now, Froggy, this is a secret.'

Froggy's eye's widened. 'Oooo! It's a secret. Shush. Don't tell Mammy.'

Sparrow held Froggy's shoulders at arm's length and looked sternly into his face. 'Don't tell anyone, nobody, understand?'

Froggy nodded. 'Nobody, don't tell nobody. And Mammy!'

'Yeh okay, nobody and Mammy. Now, Froggy, what day is tomorrow?'

'Mundey!' Froggy answered.

Sparrow smiled at him. 'That's right. And in two days' time what day will it be?'

Froggy began to count on his fingers. 'Wensdy?'

'Yes, that's right. Good man, Froggy. Now, on Wednesday I want you to go up to my house. Eileen will give you a bag. Bring the bag back here and put it in your locker and don't give it to anyone until you see me. Do you understand that, Froggy?'

'Wensdy. Get the bag off Eileen. Keep in me locker, for you, for Spawoo.'

Sparrow hugged him. 'You're a good man, Froggy. And don't tell anyone!'

Froggy put a finger to his lips. 'Shush, it's a secret.'

Sparrow stood up, followed by Froggy. Together they walked to the door. Sparrow unlocked it and opened it cautiously. He carefully looked right and left, turned to Froggy and whispered, 'The coast is clear, see yeh, Froggy.'

Sparrow left, closing the door behind him. Froggy pulled off the gloves and tossed them on the floor. He walked to his hook on the wall and put on his large overcoat. As he got to the door Froggy switched off the remaining four lights. He opened the door. He looked left and right and whispered back into the room to nobody, 'The coast is clear, shush, don't tell Mammy.' Froggy left.

* * *

Wilmount House, Malahide, 11.30pm

As one would expect, the success of Snuggstown's most notorious criminal was reflected in the luxury of his surroundings. Wilmount House was a two-hundred-year-old country mansion build by Lord Percivil Wilmount. The land had not originally belonged to Lord Percivil; it had been the property of his cousin Thomas, Earl of Dunshaughlin. But with a carefully planned plot in March of seventeen ninety, Lord Percivil Wilmount arranged the assassination of his cousin, thus inheriting all the lands. So it was that the lands upon which Wilmount House had been built were acquired through conspiracy, skulduggery, and murder. Simon Williams must have felt right at home.

Angie Williams wasn't so keen on the place. Coming from a council flat, a mansion takes some effort to get used to. Angie never bothered making the effort and confined her living space to the kitchen, one sitting room, and her bedroom. There were eight other bedrooms and copious other rooms downstairs, most of which Angie never saw from one week to the next. Around the main building of the house were numerous outer buildings, most of which were never used. That the house was not used to its full extent never bothered Simon, all he was concerned with was that he owned it. Simon was happy there, usually.

He wasn't so happy tonight. Simon prided himself on remaining cool and calm, no matter how hairy situations got. This was because Simon was usually in control. In the case of Sparrow McCabe, though, Simon wasn't in control any more. If Kieran Clancy managed to find Sparrow before Simon did, and got him to talk, Simon knew the game would be up. All he had worked for, all he had strived for, would be gone. He tried to reason the situation in his head. If Sparrow was going to talk to the police voluntarily he would have surrendered himself by now.

Simon was sitting at the kitchen table mulling all this over, and sitting in front of him was a cold cup of coffee and an overflowing ashtray. He heard Angie before he saw her. Angie had been having a bath and she was now making her way down the stairs to the kitchen. She was singing 'Hands up, baby, hands up, Give me your heart, gimmie, gimmie.' She came into the kitchen.

'You look dreadful!' Angie commented as she walked past Simon. She pushed open the door of the utility room and threw in the bundle of washing she was carrying. It didn't land in any particular place, more all over the place. Angie's maids and cleaners were well used to picking up after her. She closed the utility room door.

'D'yeh want a hot cup of coffee?' she asked Simon as she flicked the kettle on. Simon simply grunted. 'Is that a yes or a no?'

'Yes, fuckin' yes!' Simon snapped.

'Jaysus, who stole your marbles?' Angie said as she stretched to the cupboard to take out two fresh mugs.

'Sparrow McCabe,' Simon said through clenched teeth.

'Oh him, that little shit!'

Slowly Simon turned in his chair to look at this wife of his. She was unscrewing the top of a coffee jar cautiously, as if afraid to break a finger nail. He spoke slowly and deliberately. 'That little shit, as you call him, can put me behind bars if we don't find him quickly. And if I go inside, Angie dear, you go back to your mother's, because I'm fucked if I'm gonna be inside at the government's pleasure while you're out here enjoying all of this.' Simon waved a hand around the room as if everything he owned were in that room.

'Well, excuse me for breathin'!' Angie retorted. While she made the two cups of coffee and padded around the kitchen in her bare feet there was no more conversation between the two. It wasn't until she had placed Simon's mug in front of him and sat on the far side of the table with her own mug, and lit a cigarette, that she spoke again.

'Well, if you can't get to him, why don't you make him come to you?' she said, and scrunched up her face trying to get the top off a nail-varnish bottle.

Simon looked carefully at Angie. He knew full well that

the woman he had married was a complete bimbo. But having said that, sometimes, just sometimes, she came out with a little gem. So Simon pursued her thoughts.

'What do you mean, Angie love?'

'Go after his wife and his kid. That'll flush him out, wherever he is.'

Slowly Simon smiled. He really had married the most selfish bitch in the world. She was right! He got up and went to the kitchen counter where the telephone was. He punched in the number at the other end of which he knew Teddy Morgan would be. The phone rang; he waited. As he waited he looked at his reflection in the window. I'm not bad, he thought, for fifty-two. He ran his fingers through his hair.

***

Sparrow McCabe was three days on the run before he decided on his final hiding place. He spent the first three nights in doorways and alleys, but never sleeping, afraid that somebody would stumble upon him. He knew he would have to get somewhere that was safe and secure. Somewhere dry, if not warm. And somewhere that the police or Simon Williams would never think of looking.

This shed was the perfect place. It was secure, as the door had a bolt on the inside, a good strong bolt. On his first night there Sparrow had scouted the entire area to plan his escape route should the door be assaulted. He stood on one of the bare beams and loosened four tiles in the roof in readiness for a quick escape, although he believed no-one would actually look there. From the small, two-foot by two-foot window in the shed he could see the main house. Naturally, if anyone were going to call to the place they would call to the main house first; this would give Sparrow an opportunity to use his escape route long before they even thought of looking in the shed.

There was an old armchair and a hard kitchen chair in the shed. He slept in the armchair with his feet up on the hard chair. He watched every morning as the staff of the main house let themselves in. There were five staff. Two cleaners, two maids and one laundry woman. Betty, one of the maids, was the boss, and you could see by her movements that she liked being boss. When the staff would arrive every morning Betty would take the door-key from under the back door mat, insert it in the door, and then Sparrow could see her hurry through the kitchen to get to the alarm panel and punch in the code. Betty had thirty seconds to do this before the alarm went off, but she ran anyway, not realising how long thirty seconds actually was. Once the alarm code had been entered, the rest of the staff would follow her into the house. The alarm code was four, five, one, three, the first four digits of the house-owner's phone. Sparrow knew this.

Sometimes, before the staff arrived, Sparrow would slip across to the big house. He would let himself in, turn off the alarm and raid the fridge. After a hearty breakfast he would leave the dishes on the table exactly as they were, for the maids would clean up after him when they came. He would then reset the alarm and leave.

Sparrow was looking out of the shed window this night, waiting for the occupants of the house to go to bed. Not until the entire house was in darkness would Sparrow sleep, just in case. As he watched now he could see Simple Simon standing at the kitchen sink, looking at his reflection in the window and running his fingers through his hair. Sparrow smiled to himself and thought: He'll never think of looking here.

CHAPTER ELEVEN

Tuesday, 24 December
The Coffey home, Snuggstown, 9.15pm

'IT'S SNOWIN', IT'S SNOWIN!' Mickey called as he burst into his Granny's kitchen. Eileen was standing at the sink washing dishes after a late tea, and her mother Dolly was drying. Dolly leaned over and looked out the kitchen window.

'So it is, love!' She caressed the boy's head and smiled.

The snow was falling lightly outside, the final ingredient of a perfect Christmas, Eileen thought, though it was far from perfect for her. The last contact she had had with Sparrow was that phone call when he asked her to pack a duffle bag and give it to Froggy. The following Wednesday Froggy had collected the duffle bag in silence. She had not heard from Sparrow since and she prayed he was all right. But if he was out in this he'd have a hard time. Young Mickey ran out of the kitchen again and into the front room where he could kneel up on the back of an armchair and watch the snow falling under the light of the street lamps outside Dolly's home.

131

'Christmas Eve and that child with a father on the run. I don't know how you put up with that little shit-bag!' Dolly said, the dishes clattering as she put them away.

Eileen had had this goading for the last fourteen days. Each time her mother started on it, Eileen defended her husband, but it was wearing her down.

'He's not a shit-bag, Mammy. He's my husband, and I love him, believe it or not!'

'Well, if love is blind, you need a white stick.'

Young Mickey burst into the kitchen again. 'Ma! If the snow sticks tomorrow can I build a snowman?'

'Of course you can, love,' Eileen answered without even turning to the child. As quickly as he had entered Mickey left again.

'He's a gangster, that's what he is,' Dolly renewed the attack.

'He's no gangster, Mammy, you know that and I know that,' Eileen replied as she put the last plate on the draining board. She picked up a towel and began to wipe her hands.

'Then why was he working for Simon Williams?' Dolly asked pointedly.

Eileen looked at her, fury in her eyes. 'Because nobody else would give him a job, that's why!' Then she calmed down. 'Look, Mammy, just drop it, will yeh?' She sat down at the kitchen table and reached for her cigarette packet.

'I'm tellin' yeh – the sooner yeh leave that tramp the better! He's no good for yeh! He's no good for anyone and I don't care what yeh say, he is a gangster!' Dolly threw down the tea-towel on the table.

'My Dad is not a gangster!' It was Mickey, standing in the kitchen doorway.

Dolly clipped Mickey across the ear. 'Shut up you, big ears! Or Santa Claus won't come to yeh!'

'Mammy, for God's sake!' Eileen said as she went to her son and gave him a hug. 'It's all right, Mickey, Granny's just upset, that's all. Go on into the front room and watch the snow falling.'

'I haven't got big ears,' Mickey said defiantly as he made his way to the front room.

'Yeh have!' Dolly called after him.

Eileen sat down, exasperated. 'D'yeh know, sometimes, Mammy, you're a bigger kid than he is!'

* * *

The black Jaguar slowed and eventually came to a stop across the road from Mrs Coffey's house on Eagle Grove. It was quiet on the street, the only sound being the soft purr of the car engine and the swish of the wiper blades.

'Is that it?' Teddy asked.

'Yeh, that's it. She's staying there with her mother!' Bubbles replied.

Teddy was unsure, as Bubbles wasn't exactly the most reliable for intelligence. Suddenly at the front-room window he saw a boy's face. There was no mistaking whose son this was.

'Yeh. There's the boy!' Teddy said, confirming Bubbles's intelligence. The smell of petrol in the car was sickening. Bubbles turned the milk bottle upside-down to make sure the petrol soaked well into the wick.

'Go on, now!' Teddy ordered.

Bubbles left the car.

* * *

From where Eileen was sitting at the kitchen table she could see right out to the front door. Through the bubbled glass window in the door she noticed what seemed like a tiny light in the distance. It began to tumble in the air. Seeing the puzzled look on her daughter's face Dolly turned to look too. Just as she did there was a thud as something hit it, and then a whoosh as the door became engulfed in flames.

'MICKEY!' Eileen screamed. She ran to the front room. Passing the front door she could feel the heat on the side of her face. She grabbed Mickey under one arm and began to half-carry, half-drag him out of the room. As she re-entered the hall the heat shattered the window. Shards of glass went everywhere as it exploded. When she got to the kitchen Dolly was standing, frozen, staring at the front door.

'Get out, Mammy,' Eileen screamed and pushed her mother towards the back door. Within seconds they were in the back garden. Mickey was crying. By the time they made their way around to the front of the house some of Mrs Coffey's neighbours had already vaulted into the garden and were beating at the flames with old clothing. Nearly as quickly as they had started, the flames began to die. The front of the house was blackened up as far as the bedroom windows. The paint on the front door had bubbled and scorched, but there seemed to be no permanent damage done. The broken window could easily be replaced. Eileen and Dolly stood in the front garden holding the boy between them. Dolly was looking at her flame-damaged home. Eileen was looking out to the street.

'Oh my God!' Dolly said, with a tremor in her voice.

'The bastards!' Eileen mumbled as she watched the dark Jaguar drive slowly past the house.

* * *

The McCabe home, Snuggstown, 11.30pm

Kieran Clancy was sitting at the table in the McCabe sitting room. Michael Malone was in the armchair. Malone leaned over to the fireplace and placed another few lumps of coal on the newly lit fire. They both stood up as Eileen entered the room.

'Is he okay?' Kieran asked.

'He's gone off to sleep. I'm not sure whether he got a fright or whether he's just afraid that Santa won't come tonight because he's changed houses at such short notice.' Eileen gave a tiny smile.

'Kids! They're unbelievable.' Kieran laughed.

Eileen just nodded.

'What about you, are you all right?' Kieran asked.

'Yeh, I'm fine, I suppose. Did you light that fire?' she asked.

'I thought it might warm the house up a bit.' Kieran sounded almost apologetic.

'It does, thanks,' Eileen replied, a little confused now as to whether this man was friend or foe.

Kieran sat back down at the table. Eileen didn't know what to do next.

'Listen, Detective Clancy, I've told you all I can. You can go now if you like. I'm sure you have better things to be doin' on Christmas Eve?' she suggested.

'Well, I'll tell you the way it is, Mrs McCabe. I have a man coming here at about 5am. I'm going to try and have somebody here with you around the clock, so we'll stay until five.'

She looked at Michael Malone and he was nodding in agreement. 'Don't you men have families?' she asked.

'Kieran has, but not me.' Michael sounded like it was a gift to not have a family.

Eileen looked at Kieran. 'Two daughters. Seven and four.' Kieran smiled and looked at his watch. 'As long as I'm home before Santa arrives I should be all right.'

'We'll try not to get in your way,' he added, again sounding almost apologetic.

Eileen relaxed a little. 'Okay. Would the two of you like tea?' she offered.

'I wouldn't mind,' Kieran replied.

As Eileen went to make her way to the kitchen Michael asked, 'Mrs McCabe? Would you mind if I turned on the TV?'

'Not at all, the remote's over there.' She pointed to the mantelpiece.

* * *

Sparrow knew these bushes very well. And why wouldn't he, they were his bushes, at the end of his garden. He had planted them and nurtured them, and now for the first time he was using them. Even though the curtains were drawn he could see that there was light in the sitting room. Suddenly the kitchen light went on and he saw Eileen walk to the kettle and begin to fill it. Instinctively he wanted to call out her name, but knew he couldn't. He swallowed hard and held back tears. He crouched and darted across the garden to the back of his shed. He crouched again, and slowly made his way to the sitting-room window. He peeped in. Through a crack in the curtains he could see Detectives Clancy and Malone. He saw Malone point the remote control at the television set; with a couple of flashes the set came alive. On the screen he could see Gay Byrne talking to Peter Ustinov. Minutes later Eileen arrived into the room carrying three mugs. She handed one to each of the policemen and put one down on the opposite side of the table to Clancy. She then left, returning seconds later with a plate of biscuits. Eileen began to nurse her cup of tea. She looked upset.

As quietly as he could, Sparrow climbed onto the garden wall and began to scale up the drainpipe. When he was level with Mickey's bedroom he looked across at the small window that was half-open. It now looked further away than it had done when he was on the ground. Sparrow got a tenuous grip on the window sill and stretched his leg to climb up. He slipped from the drainpipe and hung precariously for a few moments, expecting that any second now the back door would open and the two policemen would come out. But nothing happened.

With a great effort Sparrow scrambled up onto the windowsill. He gripped the window frame of the small window and pulled himself erect. Leaning in through the small window he undid the latch of the larger window which now swung open. Silently Sparrow slipped in through the window, through the curtains and gently put his feet on the floor of his son's bedroom. Mickey was curled up in the foetal position, sound asleep. Quietly Sparrow sat on the edge of Mickey's bed and looked down at his son. He thought of how terrified his son must have been at the fire-bombing. He thought of how much a failure he had been as a father, not there to protect his child when he needed him most. He stroked Mickey's face softly. Mickey woke. Sparrow shushed him with a finger to his mouth.

'Daddy!' Mickey was delighted.

'Shush, son. Quiet now, there's people downstairs.'

'I know dad, it's the police. They're trying to catch you for shooting PJ Duff.' Like all children, Mickey spoke plainly and frankly.

'I didn't shoot anyone, son. They think I did and they're wrong. Believe me, I wouldn't hurt anyone, son. I just wanted to see you tonight and say Merry Christmas!'

* * *

Downstairs the two detectives were watching the television. Eileen was not paying too much attention to it, instead going over in her head the options for the future of her family. None of the options was attractive. For some reason Kieran Clancy looked at the ceiling. He stood up.

'Can I use your bathroom?' he asked.

Eileen was startled out of her reverie. 'What? Oh yeh, it's upstairs.'

Virtually on tiptoe Kieran made his way up the stairs to the landing. The bathroom door was open but instead Kieran looked at the door of Mickey's bedroom. Slowly he went to the bedroom door, and quietly and gently turned the handle to open the door a crack. He saw Sparrow McCabe sitting on the edge of the bed with his son. He listened.

'Daddy, are you a good guy or a bad guy?'

'I wish it was that simple, son. But I think I'm a good guy. What do you think?'

Mickey sat up and puts his arms around his father's neck, squeezing him tightly. 'I think you're a good guy too, Daddy!' he said.

Gently Sparrow pushed Mickey back down and pulled the covers up to his neck. Then he looked over at the bedroom door and saw the detective. The two men stared at each other.

Mickey was still gazing at his father's face, his view of the door blocked by Sparrow's body. 'Daddy, are you home for good now?' he asked.

'Not yet, son,' Sparrow replied. 'Not yet.'

The two men stared at each other again. Slowly and quietly Kieran closed the door. Without using the bathroom he returned down the stairs and entered the sitting room. He went back to the table and sat down. He took a sip from his mug of tea. Michael Malone looked up at him. 'Everything okay, Kieran?'

'Yes, Michael. Everything's okay.' Kieran took another sip from his mug of tea and quietly spoke to himself, 'Merry Christmas, Sparrow.'

CHAPTER TWELVE

EVEN THOUGH IT WAS A BANK HOLIDAY, St Stephen's Day was still boozing time, and certainly didn't bring out the boxers. Nobody turned up at the club to work out. Undeterred, Froggy opened up as usual and swept around the gym, even though the place had not been used since the last time Froggy had swept it.

Froggy didn't recognise the two men in suits who arrived into the club. Still, he smiled his welcoming smile.

'Hawoo,' he said. Leaning the brush against the wall Froggy went over to the two men, his hand extended. Had he known them he would have given them a hug as he did everybody he knew, but for now the men would have to settle for a handshake.

Neither of the Morgan brothers took Froggy's hand. Instead, Bubbles mimicked Froggy by returning his 'Hawoo' and adding 'cabbage!' The two brothers laughed. So Froggy laughed.

'Who are you?' Teddy asked, the smile gone from his face and the laughter gone from his voice.

'Froggy, hawoo,' Froggy again offered his hand.

Teddy slapped Froggy's hand down. 'Where's Sparrow McCabe?' he asked.

Froggy put a finger to his lips. 'Shush, it's a secret, don't tell Mammy.'

* * *

From his vantage point in the shop doorway across the street from St Thomas's Boxing Club, Sparrow could see the Jaguar parked outside. He knew Froggy was a creature of routine and would be there to open the club. He hadn't expected anybody else to arrive, of course, least of all the Morgan brothers. It was typical of those dopey brothers, he thought, to imagine that Sparrow would hide out in the club. The street was coated with about an inch of snow. The only tyre marks on the street were those of the Jaguar.

Sparrow waited in the doorway for twenty minutes before he saw the Morgan brothers exit. They were both laughing. Before they got into the car Bubbles said something to Teddy. They both laughed again. Sparrow watched them climb into the Jaguar and drive away. He waited another five minutes before crossing the street and slipping into the club. The main gym was empty. Sparrow stretched up and put the inside bolt on the door. He began to weave his way through the punch bags.

'Froggy! Hello, Froggy, are yeh here?' Sparrow called. Carefully Sparrow made his way through the club, room by room. There was no sign of anyone. Then he heard a very low moaning sound from the showers. He rushed in to find Froggy lying in the basin of one of the cubicles. He was naked. The bruises along his back were clearly made by the handle of the brush that Froggy used to sweep the floor every day. His right eye was swollen and closed and two of his teeth were missing. The blood from his burst lip was running down his face and into the shower basin, diluting under the running shower before going down the plughole. Pale and shaking, Sparrow bent down and hugged Froggy.

'Froggy, Jesus Christ! Froggy,' Sparrow whispered to him quietly.

Froggy grasped Sparrow and clung tightly to him. 'Spawoo, I didn't tell anyone! It's a secret ... shush, don't tell Mammy.' He whispered because Sparrow had whispered.

For fourteen years Sparrow McCabe had known he didn't have what it took to finish a job. For fourteen years he had kept his head down, living with this shame, saying as little as possible and just getting through life day-by-day. For fourteen years Sparrow had been running from his failure in Madrid, from what he saw as a failure in his very being. For the last eighteen days he had been running – from the police, from Simon Williams, from the Morgan brothers. Now, at this moment, Sparrow realised he had been a worm for the past fourteen years. He had been content to allow the Simple Simons of this world to take whatever they wanted, and for himself to be happy with whatever crumbs were thrown his way. As he held this innocent man in his arms he could feel his pain and his hurt bubble over. The worm was about to turn.

***Serious Crime Room, Snuggstown Police Station,
11.30am***

Ned Connolly and his wife had called to their daughter's for
the customary St Stephen's Day visit. After greeting his
grandchildren and presenting them with their Christmas
gifts, Ned had one quick drink, then decided to drop down
to Snuggstown's police station to visit his son-in-law. He was
not surprised that Kieran was working today, for he knew
that when a detective gets hold of a case it becomes more
than the pursuit of justice, the righting of a wrong, it
becomes personal. In his day, Ned had been that kind of
detective. If the truth be told, he wished today he was still
that detective, for he regarded what his son-in-law was doing
as real police work. But this wasn't just any old case. Simon
Williams had been a slippery fish for many years. He had a
finger in many pies and some of them very legitimate pies, as
well as being politically connected.

He offered his advice to his son-in-law as he sat across
from Kieran at his desk. He meant it only as a caution, but
Kieran took it as an accusation.

'You know Williams is behind it, I know Williams is
behind it , so just leave me at it and I'll *prove* he's behind it!'
Kieran tapped his finger firmly on the desk as he spoke.

'I'm just saying tread carefully!' Ned said.

'I heard what you said. But listen, Ned, I'll tread
whatever way I have to tread to lift this bastard. He's a cool
customer all right. But I can ruffle him; I have to shake the
tree to see what falls out. I know if I can get him flustered, if

I can get him into a panic, he'll make the wrong move and I'll grab him.' The personal nature of this case had heightened for Kieran since he'd met Eileen and Mickey McCabe. Here was a family whose entire world had been upturned just to accommodate the aspirations of a scumbag. Yes, it was personal.

The Commissioner raised his arm, the palm of his hand facing Kieran as if he were on point duty and halting traffic. 'Yes, but on the way you're stepping on a lot of toes. I must remind you, Williams has a lot of interests, there are a lot of people, big people, who would be upset if we just ruffle his feathers and then can't prove anything.'

Kieran sat up. 'Are there now? Tell me, Ned, are you one of them?'

Ned's face went red with anger. Slowly he stood up and stared down at his son-in-law. 'Don't you even suggest that!' he growled.

'Then you've nothing to worry about, Ned!' Kieran wasn't backing down.

Ned went to the coat rack where he'd left his coat. He put it on, fitted on his cap and began to make his way from the room without further comment. Kieran realised what he'd done.

'I'm sorry, Ned,' he said. 'I didn't mean that.'

Slowly Ned turned to face Kieran again. There was anger in his face at first, then he bowed his head.

Kieran went to him and laid a hand on his arm. 'Leave it with me, Ned. I swear to you I'll take him. Clean as a whistle.'

Ned looked up into his son-in-law's face – God how he wished he were in his shoes. 'It had better be clean, Kieran, squeaky clean. If you march Simon Williams into a courtroom you'd better make sure he doesn't march out again. Otherwise you and I could be looking for our own window-cleaning round.'

For a moment the two men looked at each other. Then the door swung open, banging into the heels of the Commissioner. Malone stepped in and, realising what he had done, became flustered.

'Oh Jesus! Commissioner! I mean Sir, I mean ...'

'It's okay, Michael, I've been hit by worse!' Ned laughed. 'I'll leave you to it!'

Michael breathed a sigh of relief when he had gone. 'Wouldn't that be just my luck, dumped out of the force for hitting a commissioner with a door.' The two men laughed.

'What has you in such a flap anyway?' Kieran asked as he went back to his desk.

'There's a phone call for you,' Michael said.

'Who is it?'

'He wouldn't say. He said he wanted to talk to you. D'you think is it ...?' Michael didn't even have to say Sparrow's name.

'It wouldn't surprise me,' Kieran answered as he punched the button on his phone. When he had the line he simply said, 'Sparrow?'

'How did you know it was me?'

'I thought it would be. Are you okay?' Kieran smiled towards Michael.

'Am I okay? You couldn't give a shit how I am!'

'On the contrary, Sparrow McCabe, I do care how you are. You might not know me but believe me I know you. And I'm a fan!' There was silence on the other end for a few moments.

'*You want to catch Williams?*' Sparrow asked then.

'That's the whole point of the exercise.' Kieran's heart was thumping now.

'*Okay then, I'll help.*'

'Good. You tell me where you are, I'll get you picked up, we'll get him into court and we'll nail him!' Michael reached for a pen and pad. Even he could hear Sparrow's laughter.

'*Are you serious? Do you think that on my testimony alone you could nail Simon Williams? Grow up. You've about as much chance of putting Williams in jail with the evidence you have as you have of shoving butter up a porcupine's arse with a hot needle. No. We do it my way!*'

Again there was silence for a couple of moments. Kieran pushed the pad and pen away from him and leaned back.

'Okay, Sparrow. I'm listening.'

'*Not now. Not on the phone.*'

'Okay then. Where and when?'

'*I'll call yeh back.*' The phone went dead. Kieran replaced it in its cradle.

'Well?' Michael was as anxious as Kieran.

'He's going to call me back. We'll have to wait.' Kieran put his head in his hands.

'Well, hello there,' he suddenly heard Michael call and he looked up. Moya was standing at the office door with the two children. Kieran stood up and moved towards them.

'Moya? Hi, kids.' The children ran to Kieran, and he picked them up and hugged them.

'Your children wanted to say hello to you on St Stephen's Day,' Moya announced somewhat coldly.

'I know, love, I'm sorry I missed –' Kieran began, but was interrupted by Michael.

'Hey, guys, want to see the computer room?' he said to the children.

'Yes, Michael,' they answered in unison and ran after him.

'Thanks, Michael,' Kieran called.

With the children gone Moya was not afraid to show she was upset. She sat in the chair that minutes before had been occupied by her father.

'I've seen this before, Kieran. Year after year, Daddy missing, never there. Christmas was something Mum and the family did together, but not Daddy. Oh he would pop in and out for brief visits, but there was always something going on, always somebody who needed more attention than his family. Kieran, I ask you, who needs more attention today than your kids and me?'

Kieran went over to Moya, got down on his hunkers and took her hand. 'Sparrow McCabe does. Right in the middle of Snuggstown, Moya, is a woman with a young boy and they're terrified. They're terrified because already somebody tried to burn down their home. The boy thinks he'll never see his father again. Not just this Christmas but never again. I don't expect you to understand it, Moya, but I can make the difference.'

Moya shook away his hand angrily. 'Oh, Superman now, are you?'

Kieran's tone remained level. 'No, Moya, not Superman. Just a policeman. It's all I ever wanted to be, Moya, a policeman, someone who could make a difference. Oh, I know in the big picture I make feck-all difference, but to a woman and child in Snuggstown and a man on the run, in their world, I can. A big difference.'

147

Moya burst into tears. Kieran crouched beside her again, and tried to hug her. He was surprised but glad when she hugged him back. Abruptly Moya stood up and took out a tissue, dabbing her eyes.

'Okay, all right. Once and for all I agree I'll be a policeman's wife. You make the difference, Kieran, and I'll make the home. I'm doing my best, Kieran, this is all so hard.'

Kieran put his hand on her shoulder, and she turned and looked at him. 'I know, but it will get easier. And I love you, Moya, you know that,' he said.

Moya smiled at him. 'And I love you too, Kieran, that's the problem.'

Together they left the office and went to find Michael, who had the children sitting on a desk making a chain of paper clips about six feet long. Kieran gave both children a big hug and gave them a coin each.

As they left, Kieran heard the phone ringing in his office. Some of the uniformed policemen working at the front desk looked up as the two men ran to the Special Crime Squad office. Kieran snatched up the phone.

'Yes?'

He picked up his pen and began to scribble on a pad, repeating the instructions he was hearing.

'Midday tomorrow at the Wellington Monument in the Phoenix Park? I've got it!' Slowly Kieran put down the phone.

'Was that him?' Michael asked.

Kieran nodded, but had a puzzled look on his face.

'What's up?' Michael asked.

'Where – and why – would I get a black suit?'

CHAPTER THIRTEEN

Friday, 27 December
The Wellington Monument, Phoenix Park, 10am

KIERAN WALKED ALONG THE TARRED PATH beside the monument. He scanned his surroundings. At this hour of the morning the park was populated by joggers, cyclists or dog walkers. Not far from the Wellington Monument was St Mary's Hospital, specifically for members of the armed forces. Here and there elderly or injured soldiers were out walking, each of them accompanied by a nurse. Kieran felt uncomfortable. The short collar of the white dinner shirt he was wearing was cutting into his neck and the elastic bow-tie didn't help. The black suit he had managed to get hold of had satin lapels and, to all intents and purposes, Kieran looked like a head waiter in search of a restaurant to work in.

Kieran directed his interest to a string of joggers coming towards him. In front were two women running together, one in a grey track suit, the other in lycra shorts. She must be freezing, Kieran thought. Behind them was a guy wearing a shell suit. The hood was up and under it he had a towel wrapped around his head. As he came level with Kieran he stopped. Only his nose was visible, until he pulled the towel back slightly to reveal his face. It was Sparrow McCabe.

Sparrow looked Kieran up and down. 'Are you going out somewhere?' he asked.

'You said wear a black suit, didn't you?' Kieran answered.

Sparrow folded his arms in front of his chest and began to laugh. 'I said a fuckin' track suit, ye eejit.'

'Oh! You know, I thought it was a bit odd!'

Sparrow stared at this man for a moment with his hands on his hips. 'And you're goin' to save my fuckin' life!' Sparrow shook his head. Closing the towel across his face he began to jog on a bit again, then turned back to Kieran.

'Come on, so, are you right?'

Kieran wasn't moving. 'You don't expect me to jog like this, do you?'

Sparrow stopped. 'No, I suppose not. Look,' Sparrow nodded towards Magazine Hill, the last remains of an underground armaments store-room left in 1922 by the British armed forces. 'There's a bench on the far side of that hill; make your way to it and I'll join you there in a few minutes.' Sparrow jogged off through the long grass.

* * *

Ten minutes later Kieran was sitting alone on the park bench. When he had first arrived there had been two old ladies chatting there. Kieran simply smiled at them and sat down. For a while they stopped their conversation and took in Kieran with bemused looks on their faces. Eventually one of them spoke to him.

'Is it a wedding?' she asked, a sparkle in her eye. 'Everybody loves a wedding,' she added.

'No,' Kieran replied.

The women went into a whispered discussion. Now it was the other's turn to speak.

'Is it a funeral?' she suggested.

Again Kieran just said, 'No.' But seeing that there was no stopping these two he added, 'Actually, I'm here to meet a man.' Kieran smiled, but the women did not. They gathered up their belongings and haughtily made their way away from the bench, but not before one of them snapped at Kieran, 'Filthy beast.' The women obviously had very narrow opinions of homosexuality.

Still, he had got rid of them, Kieran thought.

Within moments Sparrow jogged up to the bench and sat down beside him. Kieran lit a cigarette and after taking a drag he exhaled.

'So, Sparrow, what's the plan?'

Sparrow eyed this young detective. Instead of answering his question he asked one of his own.

'How come you didn't nick me when you could have in Mickey's bedroom?'

Kieran took another drag from the cigarette and looked away as he was exhaling. 'I didn't see you,' he said.

Again Sparrow just stared at the man.

Kieran turned back to Sparrow.

'So, what's the plan?' he asked again.

'Teddy Morgan killed young PJ Duff.' It was a simple

statement but the name PJ Duff nearly choked Sparrow as it came out.

'What about his brother, Bubbles?' Kieran was moving into policeman mode now they were in business.

'He did the damage to PJ's wife. It was awful.' Sparrow put his head in his hands.

'Did you hear the gunshot from outside?'

'No, I was standing beside Teddy. I would have stopped him if I'd known – I didn't know he was going to kill him. Oh shit!' Sparrow bent double, reliving the pain of it again.

'Well, that's enough to stitch those two bastards up. Will you give evidence against them?'

'Gladly. With pleasure. But they're not gonna snitch on Simple Simon. He's the one I want.' Sparrow sounded determined.

'No, I suppose not, but then again we don't have to worry, do we?' Kieran tossed away his butt and turned sideways now to face Sparrow. 'Because you have a plan, Sparrow, don't you?'

'Yeh. You're going to arrest Simon Williams with twenty-five grand in one pocket, a pound of heroin in the other pocket, and a gun in his right hand.' Sparrow obviously had it all worked out.

Kieran ran his fingers through his hair. 'You know, I read my stars this morning and it said nothing about that!'

'Don't be fuckin' smart. I'm serious. I'm going to get Williams into a little trap. But you have to help me spring it.'

Kieran sat forward on the bench. He rested his elbows on his knees, and clasped his hands together, interlocking his fingers. 'Sparrow,' he said, 'I'm not going to ask you why he'll have the money and the drugs, but tell me this – where's the gun going to be pointing when I arrest him?'

Sparrow laid his own elbows on his knees in an identical pose to Kieran's. 'At me, I think.'

'Well, this all sounds very good except for one or two things.'

'Like what?'

'For one thing, Sparrow, Williams never points a gun at anyone; he always has someone to do the job for him, usually Teddy and Bubbles.'

Sparrow nodded his head in agreement. 'I know. But that's because Williams is usually cool. But I'll ruffle him enough to get him to want to kill me himself! And you'll make sure that the Morgan brothers aren't around.'

'I can do that now. I can arrest them today,' Kieran said.

Sparrow was shaking his head. 'No, not today. Leave it till the last minute or Williams will smell a rat. He's smart, yeh know. I know what he's like, I worked for him long enough. I'll tell yeh when to pick 'em up.'

Kieran nodded. There was silence for a few moments. 'So, what's the plan? How are you going to make him angry?'

Sparrow leaned back on the bench and stared into space. 'It's time Mr Williams experienced a little bit of the terror he likes to dish out.'

CHAPTER FOURTEEN

Saturday, 28 December
Wilmount House, Malahide, 1am

IRONICALLY, SPARROW'S PLAN WAS VERY SIMILAR to Simon Williams's own plan. Having worked with Williams for six years Sparrow knew that Simon's dealings were all done by extension, at arm's length. Somebody else did Simon's collecting for him. Somebody else did his punishment beatings or killings for him. Somebody else even handed over the envelopes to those in the Snuggstown police force who were available for Simon to buy. All this, of course, meant that Simon never put himself in the firing line. If somebody was caught and sent down that was their problem. Time after time during the police investigations into beatings or murders the trail would lead in the direction of Simple Simon, but once it got close to him it went cold. For Sparrow's trap to be successful he had to get Simon involved. He had to make it personal.

From his 'safe' shed Sparrow had seen the lights of the house go off over ninety minutes ago. He felt it was safe now to make his move. He left the shed and casually strolled across the yard to the back door where he removed the maids' key from under the mat. He let himself in as he had done a few times for breakfast, and went to the alarm panel to punch in the code.

Upstairs in their bedroom Simon and Angie were sound asleep. On the bedside table on Simon's side was a digital electric alarm clock. The blue glow from the blue digital numbers provided the only light in the room.

Once Sparrow had neutralised the alarm he made his way through the door of the kitchen into the garage. He carefully negotiated the three steps down onto the garage floor and from his pocket he took a tiny torch. The beam flickered around the garage from wall to wall until eventually it landed on what Sparrow was looking for. He made his way to the electricity mains box. Stretching up, Sparrow flicked off the main switch. Upstairs the glow from the alarm clock went dead. Sparrow smiled to himself.

With the torch as his only light Sparrow re-entered the kitchen. Slowly he scanned the room with the torch. It landed on the kettle. I'll start there, he thought. He went over and switched it on. He then moved to the cooker, switching on every plate and the oven. Next he turned on the microwave. Next to it he noticed an electric mixer. He grinned. Finding the plug at the end of the mixer lead, he plugged it into a wall socket and switched the dial up to full speed. Sparrow opened the bread-bin and took out two slices of bread, put them into the toaster and jammed the handle down. Sparrow switched on the dishwasher, the dryer and the washing machine. There was a television on the kitchen counter; Sparrow switched that on and pushed the volume slide up to full. Before leaving the kitchen he turned the light switch to the on position.

Sparrow next found himself in the huge living room. There was a giant forty-six-inch television screen. Sparrow switched the television on and again moved the volume slide up to full. He moved to the CD player, and from a rack of CDs he selected Pavarotti's *Nessun Dorma*. He inserted it into the player, switched the player on and moved the volume button up to full. It was a surround-sound CD, so full blast was really full blast. As he moved through the house Sparrow switched every light switch he passed to the on position. Stealthily he made his way upstairs, switching on standard lamps as he went.

Gently Sparrow squeezed through the half-open door of Simon Williams's bedroom. Simon and Angie were sound asleep. From the dressing table Sparrow took one of Angie's lipsticks, bright red of course. Just as he left the bedroom Simon burst into a fit of coughing. Sparrow froze. There was a grunt and a fart, and Simon began to snore again. Sparrow returned down the stairs. At the bottom there was a huge wall mirror. Sparrow uncapped the lipstick and scrawled something on the mirror. With his work done, Sparrow left through the garage door. Just before exiting he flicked the main power switch back on. He then sprinted away across the gardens. Behind him the house exploded into a cacophony of sound and a burst of light.

★　★　★

156

The tiny glow of the bedside clock reappeared. But it was not alone. Simon and Angie Williams leapt from the bed, screaming. Simon dived to a wardrobe and pulled the door off its hinges as he tried to get to the shotgun he had stored there. He found the gun and made his way around to the end of the bed. He fell over a stray shoe, hit the ground and the shotgun blasted off. The dressing table mirror shattered and a hole appeared in the bedroom door. Screaming, Angie jumped into the wardrobe with the missing door.

With the house a cocktail of noise, above which Pavarotti was on the verge of bursting the speakers, Simon made his way downstairs, his shotgun at the ready. At the bottom of the stairs he stood aghast, looking at the mirror. Scrawled on it in red lipstick was the message: 'I will call you, we need to talk! Sparrow.' Simon emitted an enraged scream and blasted the mirror off the wall with the remaining cartridge in the gun.

'YOU BASTARD!' he screamed.

Even from where he was in the trees at the edge of the grounds of Simon's house, Sparrow could hear the faint echo of the scream.

'Step one!' Sparrow said aloud and disappeared into the night.

CHAPTER FIFTEEN

Monday, 30 December
Simon Williams's office, 11am

SIMON SLAMMED HIS FIST ON THE DESK. Both Morgan brothers jumped. They had never seen Simon so enraged. His face was purple and perspiration was dripping down his neck.

'He walked into my fuckin' house. The arrogant little shit!' Simon was roaring.

Bubbles took a step forward. 'Do you want us to keep an eye on the place, boss?'

Simon threw his arms in the air. 'A bit fuckin' late, Bubbles. No! We have to find him and he has to be stopped! What did the retard say?' Simon directed this question at Teddy.

Nervously Teddy answered. 'Nothin', boss, we gave him a good workin' over, but all he would say was: "Shush, don't tell Mammy." He's a bleedin' head-case!'

'What about the wife?'

'She's back in her own place now. Her mother's living

158

with her and they've two coppers in the house around the clock. We can't get near her, boss. It's this new copper, Clancy. He's an enigma.'

Bubbles, who had nothing to add, repeated Teddy's discription. 'Yeh, he's an en ... en ... he's an en ... he's a cunt!' Simon gave Bubbles a look so sharp you could shave with it.

Slowly Simon sat back in his chair. The phone on his desk rang. He picked it up and put it to his ear. 'Yes, what is it?' he barked.

Teddy leaned forward and put his hands on Simon's desk. 'Don't worry, boss, we'll find him,' he mouthed. But Simon held up his hand and motioned for Teddy to stay where he was.

'Okay, put him through,' Simon said into the mouthpiece. He put his hand over the phone. 'You mightn't have to find the fucker. I think he's just found us.'

'Sparrow, me auld pal, so, how are you?'

'Not great, Mr Williams, not great.'

'Enjoyed your little visit last night, did you? You should have hung around, we could have had coffee together.'

'I didn't like to do that, Mr Williams, but I needed to get your attention.'

'Well, you have it now, Sparrow, believe me, you have it now!'

'The cops are after me, Mr Williams, they're hot on my tail. It's this bastard Clancy!'

'Yeh, I've met the bollix. So, what are you saying?'

'I have to get out of the country, Mr Williams, I need money!'

Simon laughed into the phone. 'Don't kid yourself, Sparrow. Clancy has the airports and docks tied up as tight as a nun's knickers.'

'*I got that sorted. I can get out of here in two days' time on a cargo ship going to Panama.*'

'How much?' Simon asked.

'Give him fuck all,' Teddy interjected in a hushed tone. Simon held his hand up for silence.

'*They don't want money. They want a kilo of heroin, and I need about twenty-five grand to give meself a bit of a start once I get there.*'

Simon mulled this over for a few moments. 'A kilo? I think we can organise that. Come on up to the office and we'll sort something out.'

'*No way, Mr Williams. No disrespect, but I prefer to keep everything at arm's length. If you know what I mean.*'

'Well, that's all very well, Sparrow, but if I'm to get this merchandise to you, how am I to achieve that?' For a few moments there was silence on the other end of the line.

'*I'll meet you for a pick-up. Tomorrow night, eleven-thirty. I'll call you tomorrow evening, I'll tell you the place.*'

'Wait a minute, Sparrow, tomorrow night is fine even though it is New Year's Eve. I'm sure Angie can amuse herself. You can ring me all right, but I'll tell you the place when you ring.'

Again there was a pause. '*Okay, it's a deal. But Mr Williams?*'

'Yes, Sparrow?'

'*I've had enough of this running shit. If we don't make this drop tomorrow night my chance of getting out of the country is gone. I'm giving meself up to the cops, I can't take any more of this.*'

'Understandable, Sparrow. We'll make the drop, don't you worry. You call me here at the office tomorrow evening at nine.' He added, 'Sparrow, you're a better man than I

160

thought you were, it's a pity you have to go.'

'*Yeh. Such a pity.*'

The phone went dead in Simon's hand, and slowly he replaced it in the cradle. Simon folded his hands on his stomach, interlocking his fingers. He smiled broadly and leaned back in his chair.

'Got him!' he said.

* * *

Dublin city centre, 11.05am

Sparrow stepped from the phone booth. Kieran Clancy was standing there, waiting.

'All set?' Kieran asked.

'Yeh, all set,' Sparrow confirmed, but he was uneasy.

They began to walk along the footpath.

'I thought calling me a bastard was a bit strong!' Kieran said, feigning hurt.

Sparrow looked at him. 'You're a headcase, d'yeh know that?' he said, but it was clear that he liked the man. 'It's not over yet, Kieran, there's a couple of complications. He won't let me pick the spot.'

Kieran stopped. 'I thought he wouldn't. But that's not a problem. When you ring him and he tells you where it is, we'll know then.' Kieran made it sound easy, but Sparrow was shaking his head.

'It's not going to be that simple. If I know Simon Williams, I'll be walking around twenty-five phone boxes all over Dublin before he tells me the spot. And he'll be watching every one of them, so there's no chance of you coming with me.'

'I see what you mean.' The two men walked on a little further. 'Okay, then, what about this? When he does tell you the place, you leave that phone box, go to the nearest pub, ring my office, I'll be prowling the city in the car, they tell me and I'll head for there. How's that?'

Sparrow stopped walking. Kieran took a pull of his cigarette awaiting Sparrow's decision.

'Yeh, it should be all right, I suppose,' Sparrow said, but he didn't sound sure. Once again he had that strange sense of foreboding.

CHAPTER SIXTEEN

Tuesday, 31 December, New Year's Eve
The McCabe home, 10.15am

EILEEN KNEW THE GARDAÍ WERE JUST DOING THEIR JOB.
She knew they didn't mean to be an intrusion, and that they
were there for her protection. But they *were* an intrusion.
They sat there every day in her sitting room, which meant
that her downstairs living was basically confined to the
kitchen. Not that she wished to do anything hugely
important in the sitting room, it was just the fact that they
were there. For instance, she was now dressing young
Mickey each morning in the kitchen, where before this
would have been done in the sitting room. Obviously, at his
age, Eileen didn't have to physically dress Mickey. But he
had a habit of sleeping every night in the underwear he wore
that day, and unless she stood guard over him as he dressed
and handed him clean underwear, the same underwear
would remain on him all the next day.

　　She tossed Mickey's soiled underwear into the wash
basket and then opened the kitchen press drawer and took

out a bag of potatoes which she carried over to the sink. Time to begin lunch. Although he was fully dressed Mickey still sat at the table. As Eileen began to run water on the potatoes she glanced over her shoulder at him.

'Aren't you going out?' she asked.

Mickey simply shook his head. He's broody this morning, Eileen thought, so she just left him to his own thoughts and returned to the potatoes – and to her thoughts of Sparrow. She wondered would this whole business ever end.

As if Mickey read her thoughts he asked, 'D'yeh think will Daddy be home today?'

'I don't know, Mickey, I just don't know,' Eileen replied wistfully.

'Well, if Daddy's not here tonight, then who's going to be Sam The Black?' Mickey asked.

The tradition of Sam The Black goes back many, many years. Nobody is quite sure of its origin and it may even precede the tradition of Christmas. What happened in stories of olden times was that a dark-haired man should cross the lintel of the house on the stroke of one minute after midnight carrying a nugget of gold; this would bring luck to the house for the next year. A rural version was that the man of the house would leave before midnight and return just after midnight with something dug from the ground. He would knock three times on the door and it would be opened by the youngest female in the house. On entering, the man would present the exhumed object to the oldest female in the house and the entire family would celebrate the good fortune of an expected bumper harvest. As it evolved, it became the practise that a dark-haired man holding a lump of coal should be the first to knock at the family home immediately after midnight at the New Year.

Eileen's mother Dolly entered the kitchen just as the boy mentioned Sam The Black. Pinching his cheek, she said, 'Your Grandad, Mickey, Lord rest him, never missed a New Year's Eve. He was my Sam The Black!' She made her way towards the kettle.

'Daddy is our Sam The Black, Mammy, isn't he?' Mickey said.

Eileen simply turned and smiled at him.

'I bet yeh he comes home tonight, Mammy,' Mickey announced.

'Don't expect that, love.'

'I bet yeh he does, Mammy, I bet yeh!'

'Mickey, now stop. Daddy will be home when he can come home, but he won't be home tonight.'

'I bet yeh he does, Mam, I bet yeh, I bet yeh, I bet yeh.' Mickey was getting wildly carried away now.

Eileen dropped everything and took Mickey by the shoulders. She shook him in frustrated anger. 'Mickey, Daddy's not coming home tonight. Do you understand that, son, he's not coming home.' Eileen had tears in her eyes, and so had Mickey. It suddenly dawned on Eileen what she was doing. She stopped abruptly and hugged him tightly.

Dolly gently separated them. 'Now, son, off with yeh – out yeh go and play.'

'See yeh later, Ma,' the boy called as he left the kitchen.

Eileen had gone back to the sink but she wasn't washing anything. She just stood bent over it, sobbing.

Dolly placed her hand on her daughter's shoulder. 'It's not the child's fault, love.'

'I know, Mammy, I didn't mean to snap at him.' Eileen burst into tears. Her mother held her tightly, but the tears flowed and her voice came in big sobs that made it difficult for her to breathe. 'It's so desperate, Mammy. I'm angry with Sparrow but I love him. I just want him home, safe, and an end to all this.'

Dolly pulled her daughter's head down onto her shoulder, allowing her to snuggle into her mother's neck. 'There, there, there, I know exactly how you feel, love. Sure I loved your father, and he was a bollix as well!'

* * *

The Clancy home, 10.45am

Although it was bitterly cold outside and there was still a light covering of snow on the ground, Kieran's two little daughters were kicking a football on the patio. Typical, he thought, why won't they play football on the patio in the summer? Kids! He was sitting at the dining table with his feet on a footstool watching them. His thoughts were miles away. He had a mug of coffee on the table in front of him and slowly he was running his finger around the rim of the cup. Moya joined him with her mug of coffee and noticed the movement. She smiled to herself. She looked at his face and saw how dark and troubled it was. She gently placed her hand on his moving finger. He looked at his finger as if seeing it for the first time.

'I see you picked up some bad habits.' Moya smiled at him. Kieran smiled back.

'Yes, I wonder where I got that from?' He took a

mouthful of coffee and the two of them watched the children play.

'What's wrong?' Moya asked.

Kieran answered while still looking at the children. 'I've just been thinking about Sparrow. Fifteen years ago he had the world at his feet. I can remember it vividly. I'd been with you that night and I was driving back to Cavan. I was listening to the fight on the radio. He was tiny, bursting with energy and action. I remember the commentator said he seemed to glide across the ring. I'd seen him box here in Ireland, well not actually in reality, but on TV. I saw him out-pace, out-manoeuvre and out-box opponent after opponent.'

Moya looked at Kieran. 'Was he really that good?'

'He was. The best I've ever seen.' Kieran took another sip from his mug. Out on the patio, Claire was trying to teach Mary how to 'head' a ball. Claire would toss the ball in the air and the sight of Mary with her eyes clenched shut and her hands outstretched, nowhere near the ball when it came down, made both Kieran and Moya chuckle.

'How can a man, just an inch from heaven, end up so badly?' Kieran mused.

'Yes, it's hard to believe. It's really strange if he had that kind of talent,' Moya agreed.

'Oh, he had the talent, Moya. Maybe he just didn't get the breaks? I mean look at us, Moya. Sparrow has a wife, I have a wife. And Sparrow has a good wife – she's a great woman, Moya, I really mean that, she's a really good sort. And his kid shows all the signs of a good rearing. And yet he's on his knees and we're doing well. How come?'

'I hope you're not on a guilt trip here, Kieran?'

'No, no.' Kieran laughed. 'Everything we have we deserve, Moya. God knows, we've both worked hard for it. There's just that something in his eyes. I saw it that night in the bedroom with his kid. And again when I talked to him; I see it every time I talk to him. A look of resignation. It's as if he believes this is what he was always meant to be, and no more. Ah, I don't know, Moya, I'm just rambling aloud, love.' Kieran stretched his arm across the table, took Moya's hand and squeezed it.

'I take it we're not going out to celebrate New Year's Eve tonight then?' Moya asked, already knowing the answer.

'No, love, not this year. Tonight I have work to do.' Kieran bit down on his bottom lip.

Moya squeezed his hand. 'Do you think you might be able to put a sparkle back in an ex-boxer's eyes?' she asked.

Slowly Kieran turned and looked at his wife. 'It's a nice thought.'

Moya lifted Kieran's hand to her lips and kissed it. 'Yes, Kieran, it is a nice thought.'

* * *

St Thomas's Boxing Club, 12 noon

Sparrow had let himself in with his own key. They made a big thing about this, giving you your own key to the gym. It was presented to you only if you had done something special, acquired some honour for the club. Sparrow was special. He must be, he thought now, as he sat on a bench alone in the empty club, staring at the largest portrait on the

168

wall, staring at himself in his heyday. Usually he hated this portrait. Day after day working out in the gym he would have to pass it on his way from the locker room. He always made a great effort to pass by without even a glance at it. It was as if he felt the honour was undeserved.

Today he didn't feel like that. He stared proudly at the portrait. For the first time since PJ Duff's murder, Sparrow, in the quiet of the club, felt at peace. Having moved out of his previous accommodation in Simon Williams's shed, Sparrow had had to resort once again to back alleys and doorways. He'd had little sleep and was very tired. Specks of dust were dancing in the sun's rays. One of the rays shone across half of his face and its warmth made him feel sleepy. Suddenly he heard the door rattle; the handle was tried and a key slid into the lock. Sparrow crouched behind a locker. The lock clicked and the door opened slowly. Sparrow could hear feet shuffling and the door being closed and locked again from the inside. The shuffle got louder as it moved in his direction. Slowly he peeped out. It was Froggy, of course. Sparrow stepped forward into the rays of the sun and opened his arms wide.

'Froggy! Happy New Year!' Sparrow called.

Froggy was dressed in his old trench coat, under which he was wearing his boxing shorts and a tee-shirt. He beamed when he saw Sparrow.

'Spawoo,' he called and shuffled across the floor. He embraced Sparrow in a huge bear-hug.

Sparrow squeezed him tightly.

'Oh, that hurts,' Froggy moaned.

Sparrow stood back. 'Froggy, are you still sore?'

'Yes, Spawoo, no box today ... please.'

Sparrow laughed. 'Ah okay, Froggy. No box today.'

Froggy sat down on the bench and Sparrow joined him. He slapped Froggy on the knee. He really was glad of the company.

'You waiting for bad men come back, Spawoo?' Froggy asked.

'Well, kind of, Froggy,' Sparrow answered, and leaned back against the wall crossing his arms.

Froggy mimicked the motion and pose. 'I wait with yeh, Spawoo. We box them.'

Sparrow looked into Froggy's frowning face. 'God, I wish I had your heart, Froggy.'

'You can have it, Spawoo.'

Sparrow laughed again, and hugged Froggy.

'Oooo, Spawoo hurt me,' Froggy moaned.

* * *

Serious Crime Squad Room, Snuggstown Station, 2pm

When Kieran Clancy entered the room all eight uniformed officers present became alert. He had picked the eight carefully. Seven were officers that, on Michael Malone's recommendation, Kieran knew were safe. The eighth man had been Kieran's own choice, and one that had totally stumped Michael. It was Sergeant Muldoon.

Kieran sat at his desk, and the men stood around the room, facing him. The younger ones looked eager and excited. The group had been given the title: The Serious Crime Squad Task Force. That was enough to get their blood rushing. Except for Muldoon, who looked decidedly bored. Until Kieran announced what the purpose of the meeting was.

'Gentlemen, I'm sure you're all wondering why I've gathered you here today,' Kieran began, thinking to himself: Isn't that a line from a movie somewhere?' Michael must have had the same thought because they looked at each other and Michael frowned. Kieran went on.

'Tonight we have a very serious task on our hands. We will lay the trap once and for all to rid Snuggstown of Simon Williams.'

Sergeant Muldoon sat up so straight it was as if someone had shoved a ramrod up his arse. His eyes widened with interest.

Kieran went into the details of the operation. 'Any questions?' he asked when he had finished. There were none. 'Right! If you all hang on here we have coffee on the way – we don't do things by halves in the Serious Crime Squad.' Kieran smirked at the group and they laughed.

Muldoon stood and slowly began to make his way to the door.

'Something wrong, Sergeant Muldoon?' Kieran called out to him.

A little startled, Muldoon pointed to the door. 'I'm just going out for a piddle.'

Kieran smiled and waved his hand. 'Okay, you don't need permission for that. We're not at school.' Kieran smiled and Muldoon nervously smiled back. He left the room and went straight to the toilet where he did indeed have a piddle. When he re-emerged from the Gents, there was lots of chatter coming from the Serious Crime Squad room, but instead of going back, the Sergeant went towards his own desk. There were a couple of officers in the open-plan office, but nobody paid any attention to him. He sat down at his telephone, punched for a line and began to dial a number. The phone rang twice. There was a click, then a female voice answered. 'Hello?'

Muldoon opened his mouth to speak when the phone was snatched out of his hand. He went to stand but was restrained in his seat by a large hand on his shoulder. Commissioner Ned Connolly spoke into the mouthpiece of the phone.

'Hello! And a very Happy New Year; is that Mary O'Brien?'

'No, I'm afraid you've got the wrong number, this is Williams Wholesale Depot – sorry!'

'That's all right, a Happy New Year to you anyway,' Commissioner Connolly said, and he replaced the phone in its cradle. He still had his hand on Muldoon's shoulder. The officers who had been pretending lack of interest were now standing behind Sergeant Muldoon. They were waiting for the Commissioner to take his hand off Muldoon's shoulder so they could formally arrest him. The Commissioner kept his hand there. Slowly he squeezed it tighter and tighter until his thumb was digging firmly into Muldoon's neck muscle. When the pain was visible enough in Muldoon's face, Commissioner Connolly leaned down and said:

'And a very Happy New Year to you, Sergeant Muldoon!' Muldoon was arrested and taken to a police station thirty miles away where he would be held for questioning for twelve hours.

* * *

Blanchardstown Shopping Centre, 5pm

It had been a simple mistake. The two plainclothes detectives were furious. They were actually giving the Morgan brothers more credit for losing the tail than they deserved. All it took to break the connection between the Morgans and the detectives following them was a simple cigarette and a stroke of luck. The shopping centre was doing a brisk trade for a bank holiday. The detectives didn't mind this as it made it easier to stay out of sight. Unaware that they were being followed, the brothers sat on a bench beside the fountain in the centre of the mall. As usual, Bubbles put his hand in his pocket and extracted a packet of cigarettes. He lit one. The detectives watched as a security man approached Bubbles and indicated to him a No Smoking sign.

'Well, where am I supposed to smoke?' Bubbles asked.

'You could smoke in the café, or just outside the Gents toilet. If you go through that door and down the hallway you'll find it.' The security man was very pleasant. Grumpily the two brothers made their way through the door marked 'Gents Toilet' and stood in the hallway outside the main toilets.

The detectives looked at each other. One followed while the other waited. When the first detective went through the first two doors he saw the Morgan brothers standing in the hallway beside a large ashtray. He walked straight past the men into the Gents. After a couple of minutes he washed his hands and walked to the blow dryer rubbing his hands together while looking at the chrome nozzle in which he could see the reflection of Teddy and Bubbles still standing outside the door. When he walked back out into the hallway Teddy was halfway through his cigarette. Again the man simply strolled past them. Back in the mall he explained to his partner that the Morgans were just having a smoke, so the two sat down to wait on the bench previously occupied by Bubbles and Teddy. They waited. What they didn't know was that as they were sitting by the fountain the Morgan brothers had bumped into a friend.

It was Teddy who recognised Dick Murray. Dick was wearing grey overalls and carrying a sweeping brush. He was dressed almost identically to how he had been dressed when Teddy had last met him in Mountjoy prison. The brothers greeted Dick warmly. Beside the door to the gents toilet was another door. Nodding towards it Dick invited the two to join him in his 'office'. Dick's office was simply a store room for toilet paper, cleaning materials, and spare brushes and so on. All three went in, closed the door behind them and joined Dick in a friendly smoke and chat.

After ten minutes the detectives began to get panicky, and they both entered the hallway leading into the gents toilet. Finding the hallway bare they went into the toilet in the hope the Morgan brothers would be in there. They drew a blank. Now in a panic, they came out and went down a fire escape, as that was the only other exit from the hallway. The fire escape brought them down four floors into an open yard. There were delivery trucks all over the place, some refuse bins, and about eight points of exit from the yard. Desperate now, the two detectives split up and headed in opposite directions. It was fifteen minutes later before they met up again at the fountain in the centre of the mall. At this stage depression had taken over from panic. Almost simultaneously they came up with the idea of checking out the Morgans' car. They sprinted to the carpark. The Jaguar was gone. They tossed a coin to decide who would be the one to ring Detective Sergeant Clancy with the bad news.

* * *

Williams Wholesale Depot, 8pm

When Bubbles and Teddy entered Simon's office, Simon was leaning back in his chair with his feet up on his desk. There was an uncorked bottle of Cotes de Nuit Villages on his desk and Simon was holding a glass of it in his right hand. In his left hand he held an expensive Cuban cigar, and on his face was a large smile.

Teddy smiled at the sight. 'Well now, Mr Williams, you're celebrating early?'

'Well, it is New Year's Eve, boys. Grab yourselves a glass each!' Simon said as he rocked back and forth on his chair. The Morgan brothers took two wine glasses from a side table and made for the bottle on Simon's desk.

'Not that!' Simon barked. 'The other piss on the shelf over there.' The Morgan brothers stopped in their tracks and without question changed direction; they were happy to drink the other piss, if that's what Mr Williams wanted. They filled a glass each of the lukewarm white wine and stood by Simon's desk.

'There's our bait.' With the wine glass Williams indicated the white envelope and a tinfoil-wrapped parcel.

175

The brothers stared at the packages for some moments. They took another sip from their glasses.

'What way do you want me to handle this, Mr Williams?' Teddy asked.

But even as Teddy was asking the question Williams was shaking his head.

'No, Teddy, not this time, this time it's personal. This time I'll handle it.' The brothers looked at each other, surprise showing on their faces. Simon Williams hadn't come on a job with them in years. With the heel of his foot Simon pushed on the edge of the desk and his chair spun around to face the panoramic window. The brothers could see his reflection. He had an evil smile on his face as he spoke. 'I want to see this little bastard shit himself before I blow his fuckin' head off.'

* * *

The McCabe home, 8.45pm

Eileen brushed the hair off young Mickey's forehead. He was sound asleep. She rose from her sitting position on the bed and began to pick up his scattered clothes. When she lifted the crumpled trousers from the floor she saw beneath them a tiny Matchbox Jaguar. She lifted the toy and placed it on Mickey's bedside table. Her eye rested on the framed photograph of her husband. She picked it up and looked at it lovingly. Slowly, warm rivulets of tears flowed down her cheeks and into the side of her mouth. She held the photograph to her breast and looked out the window at the moon.

St Thomas's Boxing Club, 8.55pm

Froggy stared out the window at the moon, wondering why such a big ball never bounced. Sparrow was sitting on the bench lengthways with his feet up and his back to a locker. He was asleep. Slowly he woke, and as his eyes cleared he looked at Froggy. He jumped up with a start. Froggy too jumped up into a boxing position.

'We box them, we box them, Spawoo?' Froggy asked.

Sparrow was groggy and in a slight state of panic.

'What time is it, Froggy? Oh, it doesn't matter.' Sparrow ran down the hall past the ring and looked up at the gym clock. It was eight fifty-five.

'Shit!' Sparrow exclaimed. He turned on his heel and sprinted the length of the room to the public phone just inside the locker-room door. Rummaging through his pocket, he came up with a coin, inserted it in the phone and dialled a number. After just two short rings the phone was answered.

'Serious Crime Squad.' Clancy's voice was expectant.

'Clancy, is that you?'

'Yes, Sparrow, any news?'

'No, just checking in.'

'Well, I've got bad news, Sparrow.' Clancy's statement made the hair on the back of Sparrow's neck stand up.

'Shit! What is it? It's not Eileen or Mickey, is it?'

Clancy tried to be as calming as possible, knowing he had fucked up. 'No, no, nothing like that, it's the Morgan brothers ... I had them tailed all day but my boys lost them a few hours ago. I'm sorry, Sparrow.' The apology was genuine.

Sparrow rubbed his eyes and tried to think clearly. 'Okay, Clancy. I should have rang you earlier anyway to pick them up. Would you believe it, I fell asleep.'

There was silence between the two men for a few moments on the phone.

'So, what do you want to do? Do you want to call it off?' Clancy asked tentatively.

'No way! Tonight's the night, Clancy. It ends tonight. I wasn't joking when I told Williams I couldn't take any more of this shit. I can't.' Sparrow was emphatic.

'Okay, Sparrow, it's your call. I'm hitting the streets in a patrol car now. I'll be waiting for word.'

Sparrow hung up. With his hand still on the phone he stood for a while trying to calculate how big a difference the Morgan brothers would make. His only worry now was that with the Morgans free Williams wouldn't come. He lifted the phone, inserted a coin and dialled Williams's number. The phone was answered immediately.

'*Yes?*' The voice is unmistakably Simon's.

'Mr Williams, it's me, Sparrow.'

'*Okay, Sparrow. Where are you?*'

'Mr Williams, let's cut the shit and get on with this! This boat won't wait forever.'

'*Okay, Sparrow, let's get the ball rolling. At the corner of Parnell Street and O'Connell Street there's a phone box. I'll be ringing you there in fifteen minutes. You answer it. Now go!*'

The phone went dead in Sparrow's hand. Sparrow hung up and began to put on his jacket, then remembered Froggy. He ran to him.

'The bad men, Spawoo, we wait for the bad men?' Froggy asks.

'No, Froggy, I must go now. Later, we'll get them later,' Sparrow called as he left the club. He sprinted down the street to Carpenter's Hill. At the traffic lights he looked left and right – the street was empty. He decided to go right towards Snuggstown village. He raced down the steep hill and had difficulty stopping at the bottom. He slid to the edge of the kerb just in time to see a cab coming towards him. He hailed it. He quickly climbed into the back and slammed the door.

'The corner of O'Connell Street and Parnell Street,' he called to the driver. With total disregard for traffic coming in either direction the taxi driver made a U-turn. When he'd completed the manoeuvre and was on the road safe and sound, he called over his shoulder.

'Headin' out for the night?'

'No.' Sparrow answered, thinking: Fuck, a compulsive chatterer.

'Ah, you're right. Only fuckin' lunatics out there tonight. I used to go out all the time on New Year's Eve with me wife but yeh spend hours trying to get a drink in a bar and every smelly whore is bumping up against yeh – and half of what you're after buyin' is spillin' on the fuckin' floor – fellows are blowin' smoke in yer face, girls are pokin' handbags up yer arse, and then when midnight comes every fucker wants to hug yeh. I've no time for it meself – it's a load of shite.'

'Yeh,' Sparrow answered. When the taxi came to the junction of O'Connell Street and Parnell Street it had to stop at a red traffic light. Sparrow paid the driver and hopped out,

179

then sprinted across the junction to the telephone which was already ringing. He snatched it up. He was breathless.

'Williams!' he called into the phone.

Williams was very calm and very cool. *'Yeh, Sparrow. Your next port of call is George's Street, just outside Bewley's Café.'*

After running around to eight phone booths Sparrow had covered half of the northside of Dublin and a bit of the southside. In the square at Temple Bar, drenched with perspiration, he snatched up the ninth phone. This time he didn't introduce himself or even ask was it Williams on the other end of the line.

'I've had enough of this running-around shit, Williams. If you're not convinced by now that I'm not being followed you never will be. So let's call it off and I'll give meself up to the cops.' He spoke loudly into the phone, not caring at this stage who heard him or who didn't.

After a pause, Williams answered. *'Keep cool, Sparrow. We're happy you're not being followed. I just need to fill in a bit of time. Now, at eleven o'clock exactly I'll meet you by the bridge in Stephen's Green. Eleven o'clock, don't be late!'*

'Wait a minute, Williams, Stephen's Green is closed at this hour of the night,' Sparrow argued.

'Is it now, Sparrow? Well, I'll be there!' Williams answered.

The phone went dead in Sparrow's hand. Sparrow replaced the receiver. For a few moments he leaned against the inside of the booth to catch his breath, then he looked around for a clock. He found one at the top of a tower. It read ten-thirty.

* * *

Downtown Dublin City, 10.30pm

Kieran looked at his watch again. He sighed.

'It'll be somewhere busy, somewhere with a lot of people,' Michael Malone speculated.

Kieran just stared out the window, biting his thumb nail. 'Do you reckon?' He stretched across and picked up the microphone of the car radio.

'Task Force One to Task Force Base. Over!' There was a bit of squelch and a female voice came back.

'Go ahead, Task Force One , over.'

'Any word from Sparrow yet?' Kieran's voice was hopeful.

'No calls yet, Sir. Over!' Kieran loosened his grip on the mike and let the spiral cable snatch it back to the floor.

'Damn!' he exclaimed, going back to his nail-biting.

* * *

The McCabe home, 10.35pm

Eileen put another shovelful of coal on the fire. It was as if she was trying to make the house as warm as possible, to take the chill off her loneliness. The television was not switched on, as if she was in mourning. Dolly had left for the evening to celebrate New Year's Eve with friends. Eileen was alone now in the house but for her sleeping son upstairs. She turned on the radio and recognised the upbeat music – 'Saturday Night at the Movies', a song she and Sparrow had danced to many years before. Eileen sat into the armchair by the fire and drifted into thoughts of her husband.

* * *

Temple Bar, 10.40pm

As Sparrow made his way along Temple Bar there were revellers everywhere and an air of merriment about the place. At the corner of Exchequer Street and Parliament Street, Sparrow picked out a pub. He went in to find the place jam-packed. Everyone was singing and talking, glasses were clinking, smoke was heavy in the air. Sparrow clawed his way to the bar. When he got there he tried desperately to get the attention of a barman, but it was like trying to get a blessing from the Pope for your third marriage. Eventually a barman did catch his eye. 'What can I get ya?'

'Where's the phone?' Sparrow shouted.

'What?' the barman called, cocking a hand to his ear.

'I said, where's the phone?' The barman pointed down to the far end of the bar. Hoping that the fellow actually understood his question, Sparrow started to make his way down through the bar. As he came out of the milling crowd at the bottom he saw a wall-phone tucked under the stairs. He made his way over and inserted a coin. He dialled the number.

'*Snuggstown Detective Unit, can I help you!*' It was a female voice.

'I need to get a message to Detective Clancy. It's urgent.' Sparrow was roaring over the noise of the pub.

'He's expecting a message. Is this it?' the girl asked, to Sparrow's relief.

'Yes!'

'Go ahead then.'

'Eleven-fifteen, the bridge, Stephen's Green Park!' Sparrow called each word very deliberately.

'You'll have to speak up. I can't hear you, it's very noisy there. Can you get to a quieter phone?' Although she was in the quiet of the police station the girl was now roaring back at Sparrow. Sparrow stuck a finger in his left ear and spoke even higher than before, if that was possible.

'I'm lucky to have got to this phone, love. I said eleven-fifteen, St Stephen's Green Park. At the bridge!'

Sparrow glanced around furtively, but he didn't have to worry. Nobody was paying a blind bit of attention to him. The phone began to beep, looking for more money. Sparrow thrust his hands into his pockets, but came up without any change.

'Shit!' he exclaimed and slammed the phone back into its cradle. Again he beat his way through the milling crowd to the bar. The same barman came over.

'Are you okay, pal?' he asked.

Sparrow was just about to ask the man for change for the phone when at the other end of the bar he saw Teddy Morgan coming through the door. Teddy looked furtively around the room; he was obviously looking for Sparrow.

'I said, are you okay, pal?' the barman called again.

'Yeh. Give us a pint, pal!'

The barman went to the Guinness pump to begin to pour the pint. Although Sparrow pretended not to notice, he saw when Teddy Morgan recognised him and noticed relief in Teddy's face. Teddy called to the barman for a drink. Within a couple of moments Sparrow's pint was delivered. He paid for it, and in his change received the coins he needed for the phone. He sipped the pint standing at the bar, still pretending not to notice Teddy.

Sparrow checked his watch; it now read 10.50pm. He placed the pint on the counter and left. Heading for the door, he passed within ten feet of Teddy, but again he pretended not to notice him.

Sparrow turned right towards Dame Street, walking casually as if he was going nowhere special with nothing on his mind. After about a hundred yards Sparrow glanced over his shoulder. Behind him, maybe two hundred yards away, the dark Jaguar was crawling along the kerb. Sparrow was less than half a mile from Stephen's Green. He knew he was being followed and yet also knew he must get to a phone, for without Kieran Clancy's arrival the entire plan is fruitless. More than fruitless. It was probably going to be fatal.

* * *

Downtown Dublin, 10.50pm

'Task Force Base to Task Force One! Over.'

Both Kieran and Michael jumped as they hear the young woman's voice on the radio. Kieran called back.

'Go ahead, Task Force Base.'

'The subject has telephoned in. Over.'

'Go ahead, give me the message!'

'I'm afraid, Detective Clancy, the message was pretty garbled.

Wherever he was ringing from was very noisy but I wrote down what I think he said.'

'Sweet Jesus tonight! You'd think they'd be able to take a simple message!' Kieran roared at no-one in particular.

Michael stretched his hand across and laid it on Kieran's arm. 'Hey, Kieran, keep cool. It'll be okay.'

Kieran took a couple of deep breaths and returned to the radio. 'Give me what you have then, Task Force Base. Over.'

'He said, I think, eleven-fifteen at a bridge in some park?'

'A bridge in some park?' Kieran repeated what he'd heard to Michael as if Michael hadn't heard it.

'What park has a bridge in it?' Kieran asked again, thinking aloud.

'The Phoenix Park?' Michael asked.

'Maybe. That's where he arranged the first meeting with me. Maybe it's the Phoenix Park!' Both detectives were stumped.

'But where in the Phoenix Park is there a bridge?' Kieran asked.

'The Furry Glen,' Michael said. 'I'm sure of it.'

Kieran thought about this.

'Will we close in on the park?' Michael was ready to go into action.

'I don't know, I've a feeling if Sparrow meant the bridge in the Furry Glen he would have said the Furry Glen! I just don't know, Michael. Let me think about it!' Kieran went back to biting his thumb-nail.

* * *

Sparrow made a decision. Instead of going up Dame Street he went into George's Street and took the first left down Dame Court. As he turned into Dame Street he saw the Jaguar indicate to follow. When Sparrow turned left into Dame Court he was out of sight of the car and would be for about five or ten seconds. Immediately he rounded the bend he began to sprint. Looking over his shoulder he saw the lights turn into Dame Court. Sparrow stopped to a walking pace again. He had put a little more distance between the Jaguar and himself, and felt he'd achieved something.

Halfway up Dame Court, Sparrow took a right into Corbally Avenue, an 'S' shaped lane which would be difficult for the Jaguar to negotiate. Once again as soon as he'd taken the turn Sparrow sprinted. The distance between him and the car had now increased so much that as he turned into South Anne Street the Jaguar was just beginning to negotiate the first bend in the avenue. Sparrow took advantage of this, sprinting up South Anne Street into Drury Street and was halfway up Drury Street before he saw the lights of the Jaguar swing into South Anne Street.

Sparrow now took a sharp left into the Westbury Mall. This area was pedestrian only, and by the time he had exited at the far end of the Mall he had lost the Jaguar. As he walked along Chatham Street he searched but found no phone kiosk. He turned into Grafton Street and headed towards Stephen's Green. He checked his watch. It read 11.05pm.

Sparrow calculated that if he was lucky he would have one more chance to ring Clancy. He saw his chance. The phone kiosk was on the corner of Stephen's Green and Grafton Street just outside Pizza-Pizza. He didn't go directly to the kiosk, but instead went to the doorway of Pizza-Pizza and checked Stephen's Green in every direction, then Grafton Street in every direction. And he even waited until it was quiet on South King Street. Then staying close to the shopfronts, Sparrow made his way to the phone kiosk. He looked around carefully, then, satisfied he was in the clear, darted to the kiosk, took out a coin, and lifted the receiver. The receiver cable dangled in his hand, severed.

'Bastards!' Sparrow said aloud as he slammed down the receiver. Sparrow would not get another chance. His only hope was that the first message he gave had been understood. He headed for Stephen's Green.

* * *

Phoenix Park, 11.00pm

Michael stopped the car outside of the security hut at Áras An Uachtaráin. This beautiful building, formerly the home of the Viceroy of Ireland in the centre of the Phoenix Park was now the home of the President of Ireland. There was a twenty-four hour police guard on the building. When the two detectives pulled up in the car the guard on duty made his way from the security hut to their side window. Michael lowered his window.

'Good evening, lads, can I help you?' he asked in a heavy Dublin accent. Quickly Michael explained that they were looking for a bridge in a park and that they had taken the Phoenix Park as their best bet. But the guard shook his head.

'Well, I'll tell you where the bridges are here, but if you ask my opinion you're on the wrong track altogether.'

Kieran leaned across Michael. 'Why? Where do you think we should be looking?'

The guard took off his hat and looked thoughtful for a moment. 'Well now, if I was looking for somewhere quiet, in a park that had a bridge, I'd probably be thinking more like Stephen's Green,' he said. He didn't even have time to replace his cap before Kieran had screamed, 'Go!'

The car did a reverse handbrake turn. At full speed Michael and Kieran belted towards St Stephen's Green, four miles away.

* * *

St Stephen's Green, 11.11pm

Sparrow carefully scaled the spiked railings of St Stephen's Green Park. It had begun to snow again and the fresh blanket meant that his feet simply crunched softly as they landed. Stealthily he made his way through the bushes, crawling in places through undergrowth to a spot where he could be concealed and yet watch the bridge over the small stream that runs through the park. Sparrow crouched low and waited for some sign of life. Within minutes Sparrow heard a rustling sound in the bushes behind him. He sank lower into his hiding place. The rustling got louder as whatever it was came towards him. With the orange street lights for a backdrop, Sparrow saw a dark, shadowy figure getting closer, and closer. As the figure passed by Sparrow's hiding spot, Sparrow pounced. He placed his hand over the mouth and pulled the figure to the ground. Instinctively he drew his left arm up in the air to punch into the face. He pulled his punch just in time. It was Froggy.

'Froggy, for Christ's sake, what the fuck are you doin' here?' Sparrow eased his hand off Froggy's mouth.

Froggy looked terrified. 'I follow you. Help you. Are the bad mans comin'?'

'You shouldn't be here!' Sparrow was annoyed at this new complication.

'I help you, Spawoo. We box them?'

'No, we won't!' The thought that went through Sparrow's mind was that of all the friends he had it had to be the retarded man who was with him in his deepest moment of fear. Sparrow sagged.

Froggy sat up. 'Spawoo angry with Froggy?'

'Yes! Sparrow is angry with Froggy,' Sparrow said, trying not to sound too angry.

'Spawoo not Froggy's friend now?'

Sparrow put his arm around Froggy. 'Yes! Yes, Sparrow still Froggy's friend.'

Suddenly in the distance Sparrow heard the click of a steel heel-cap. He pushed Froggy to the ground, and crouched down low. Slowly Sparrow raised his head until he could just about make out the bridge. Three figures strolled casually down the path towards the small bridge. Froggy put his head up, but Sparrow pushed him roughly back down and put a finger to his lips. 'Shush,' he warned.

Froggy repeated the motion and the sound.

In the dim light that was bleeding in from the street lights outside the park it was hard to tell Teddy Morgan and Bubbles Morgan apart, as both were wearing dark overcoats.

But there was no doubt that the stocky man in the tan camel-hair coat with the brown velvet collar was Simon Williams. Sparrow supposed he should be delighted. It had worked, Simon was here. But instead he was terrified. There was no sound of police cars screeching up. No other noises in the bushes of Serious Task Force men stealthily making their way towards the bridge. There was no sound but the click of Simon's heel as he made his way to the bridge. The entire plan had gone badly wrong. The Morgan brothers were supposed to be incarcerated in a cell somewhere. They weren't. Kieran Clancy and his Serious Crime Squad were supposed to be here. They weren't. Froggy was not supposed to be here. He was. The whole thing was a mess.

* * *

Ormond Quay, 11.12pm

'Task Forces Two and Three, I repeat, St Stephen's Green, entrance at the Shelbourne Hotel end. Wait for me there. Over,' Kieran barked into the radio.

'I could make better speed if you'd let me use my siren and light,' Michael called to Kieran.

'No! No sirens, no lights, I don't want to scare them off!' Kieran checked his watch. It was 11.13pm. He repeated that same thought into the radio microphone. 'Task Forces Two and Three – no lights, no sirens. Over.' Both cars acknowledged receipt of Kieran's message.

'Step on it!' Kieran said to Michael.

'I have me foot to the floor, what d'you want me to do – take out a hacksaw and cut a hole in the floor?' Michael called back sarcastically to relieve the tension. In other circumstances Kieran would have laughed. Not this time. Instead he took out his pistol, checked that the cartridge was full, shoved it back up into the handle, and cocked his gun.

***

St Stephen's Green, 11.14pm

Slowly and quietly Sparrow slid out of his jacket. He handed it to Froggy.

'Froggy, do you want to help Sparrow?' he asked earnestly. Froggy simply nodded in reply.

'Okay, see this jacket, Froggy? This is an important jacket. Froggy, stay here and mind this jacket. Okay?' Again Froggy nodded. The jacket wasn't at all important, of course, what was important was that Froggy stayed exactly where he was. Sparrow had enough to worry about with his own life, he didn't need to worry about Froggy's as well.

'Stay here and mind jacket, okay?' Froggy repeated in a whisper. Sparrow curled his hand around the back of Froggy's neck and pulled Froggy's head toward his own. When they touched foreheads Sparrow patted Froggy on the side of the face. 'Good man!'

Sparrow began to crawl through the bushes for a couple of yards. When he felt he was clear of Froggy's spot and that where he had come from couldn't be detected, he made for a pathway. He then stood, brushed himself down and casually strolled over to meet the three men. On his way he glanced around. There was no sign of Detective Clancy or anybody else.

Right on the brow of the bridge the four men met face-to-face.

Teddy was the first to speak. 'Well, well. The little Sparrow is out of his nest!'

Sparrow ignored Teddy and looked directly at Simon Williams. 'Hello, Mr Williams.' He spoke casually, as if meeting Simon in a supermarket.

'Hello, Sparrow. You look a bit rough.' Williams looked very confident.

Sparrow examined himself. 'Yeh, well, I've been having it kind of rough for the last few days, if yeh know what I mean. Still, it's over now, isn't it?' As he spoke, Sparrow's eyes never left Simon's eyes. Sparrow could see the anger there.

'Indeed it is, Sparrow. Indeed it is.' Williams spoke through clenched teeth.

Sparrow took his hands from his trouser pockets and held them out by his sides. 'Sorry to bring you out on a night like tonight, Mr Williams.' Sparrow looked around while speaking, making it look as if he was checking on the weather. There was no sign of Kieran Clancy. All was quiet.

'No problem, Sparrow.' Simon took a step towards Sparrow. 'Of course, I would like to be partying with Angie, but one must take care of business first!' He sounded every inch the businessman.

'Your wife is out partying, Sparrow, in some disco, with some young fellow stuck into her!' Teddy goaded Sparrow, and both Morgan brothers laughed.

Simon raised a hand. 'Now, now boys, let's mind our manners.'

Sparrow gazed at Simon. 'That's okay, Mr Williams, yeh don't expect anything from a pig but a grunt.'

Teddy made to move at Sparrow but Simon placed his hand across Teddy's chest. 'Easy, Teddy. I'll take care of this.'

Sparrow's mind was now racing. To the left over the bridge was deep water. To the right over the bridge was also deep water. He discounted these two options as points of exit. To run back from where he came meant running at least ten to fifteen yards in a straight line. This was something Sparrow didn't particularly want to do. Between the three men they had the small bridge blocked on their side. Sparrow made the decision not to plan, but to wing it!

'So, Mr Williams, did you bring the stuff?' Sparrow asked.

'Indeed I did.' As Simon answered he dug his hands into his coat pockets. From his right-hand pocket he extracted a white envelope.

'In this pocket I have twenty-five grand.' Simon had obviously decided to do a commentary. He then extracted his left hand, in which there was a foil-wrapped parcel in a clear plastic bag.

'And in this pocket,' he was beginning to sound like a game-show host, 'one kilo of heroin!' He put the money and the heroin together in his left hand.

'Great, I knew you'd bring the stuff,' Sparrow said.

'Yes, indeed I did – but you're not getting it.'

The Morgan brothers smiled simultaneously, like synchronised swimmers.

Sparrow knew this, of course, but he played dumb.

'What d'yeh mean?' he asked, like a little kid.

Instead of answering, Simon barked at Bubbles. 'Search him, Bubbles.'

Bubbles hurriedly walked to Sparrow and began to frisk him. As he was frisking, Simon inserted his hand into an inside pocket and pulled out a revolver.

'This is what I brought for you, my little Sparrow.' The pistol had a silencer on it, giving it an exaggerated length. Without further ado Simon pointed the pistol directly at Sparrow. In one movement, as Simon was squeezing the trigger, Sparrow grabbed Bubbles and turned him to face Simon. The gun spat and two slugs buried into Bubbles's chest. Bubbles looked down at his chest and then up to Simon Williams, his face looking puzzled.

'Mr Williams?' were Bubbles's last words before he passed out. Even as his body was dropping to the ground, Sparrow had taken off like a sprinter. Teddy Morgan immediately ran after him. Simon moved to the edge of the bridge and squeezed off two more shots at Sparrow. The first one ricocheted two feet in front of Sparrow as he ran; Sparrow heard the second one whizz past his ear, giving off a little bang as it broke the sound barrier. Simon Williams, still on the bridge, had gone completely crazy now.

'Happy New Year, Sparrow! Ha, ha, ha, ha!' he bellowed into the night air. His eyes were bulging and his face red with frenzied rage.

Very clearly and sharply from out of the bushes beside the bridge came another voice.

'And a Happy New Year to you, Mr Williams!'

Simon Williams spun towards the source of the voice to find Kieran Clancy, Michael Malone and three uniformed policemen surrounding him, all five of them panting. Kieran Clancy was pointing a pistol at Simon. In his crazed frenzy, Simon raised his pistol, but too late! Kieran's gun barked off one shot. The bullet caught Simon on the shoulder, cracking his shoulder blade and tearing four inches of muscle apart as it exited. Simon Williams crumpled to the ground with a yelp.

Kieran turned to Michael. 'Michael, put handcuffs on him and stay with him. You three fan out.' He shouted to the other policemen: 'And don't shoot at anything you don't recognise!' This was good advice as the uniformed Gardaí were carrying uzi sub-machine guns, which they only got to carry twice a year, at most. As the Gardaí spread out, Kieran took off, sprinting in the direction he saw Sparrow and Teddy go.

Sparrow was running as fast as he could. As he was bursting through the bushes, they ripped at his face and tore his shirt, and red streaks appeared across his face and chest. He felt no pain. At first when he began to run he could hear Teddy Morgan cursing and swearing behind him; but now he heard nothing. He stopped and listened carefully; there was no sound. I must get to the street, he thought to himself. He began to head for where he saw lights. Within seconds he emerged into an open space. He found himself beside the bandstand in the centre of Stephen's Green. In the cover of the bandstand he stopped and began to catch his breath; this was difficult as he was crouching, his breath coming in gasps. He surveyed the damage to his clothes, which were now shredded and dirty and speckled with blood. Carefully he ran his shaking hand along the scratches on his face which were oozing blood.

Once he had his breath back he began to inch his way around the bandstand. Just as he got to the steps that led up onto the platform, he heard the metallic click of a revolver being cocked behind him. Slowly he turned. Teddy Morgan was standing no more than ten feet from him. He had a smile on his face and his right arm was extended with the pistol pointed directly at Sparrow's head.

'Tweet, fuckin' tweet,' Teddy said with a smirk.

* * *

The McCabe home, 11.19pm

Mickey was lying sound asleep in his bed. The only light in his bedroom was that which was spilling in from the landing, as the door was half open. Suddenly, like a flick-knife, the child shot up into a sitting position and screamed.

'Daddy!'

He was terrified and shaking. His mother's footsteps came pounding up the stairs. Eileen burst in the bedroom door and took Mickey in her arms.

'Mickey, are you all right?'

Mickey put his head on her shoulder and held her tightly. 'Daddy,' he said softly again.

Eileen hugged her son, rubbing her hand up and down his back. 'Shush now, Mickey, I'm sure Daddy's fine.' She took him by the hand and led him out of the bed and onto the landing.

'Come on, Mickey, let's go downstairs and turn on the television. We'll watch all the people bringing in the New Year.' She closed the bedroom door, which sent a puff of wind into the bedroom. This blew the curtains away from the window. They brushed lightly against the photograph of Sparrow and it toppled to the floor.

* * *

Bandstand, St Stephen's Green, 11.20pm

Keeping his eyes at all times on Teddy, Sparrow walked backwards up the steps of the bandstand. Teddy walked after him, keeping the distance between them. In the centre of the bandstand Sparrow stopped, his hands up like in an old cowboy movie. Teddy now walked towards him. The distance was closed down to about two yards.

'Well, Sparrow, it's over!' Teddy sneered.

'Is it, Teddy? I thought it wasn't over until the fat lady sings?' Sparrow was talking smart, but feeling terrified.

Teddy put his hand to the side of his head and cocked his ear in the air. In a mocking tone he said, 'I think I hear the fat lady clearing her throat.'

From out of the darkness came another voice.

'No, that was me. I have a cold.' It was Froggy.

Teddy glanced with a start in the direction Froggy's voice had come from. Froggy was standing two steps down on the bandstand steps. With Teddy distracted for a second, Sparrow lunged at him, slapping at his wrist. The two men grappled. The gun fell from Teddy's hand and slid across the bandstand floor towards Froggy. Froggy picked it up and looked at it as the two men wrestled on the ground.

Sparrow called out, 'Run, Froggy. Run!'

Froggy ran; he didn't know where, but he ran anyway. He headed for the bushes, where suddenly he was tripped up and floored. Froggy found himself lying on his back with an elbow in his throat. The figure standing over him held a gun to his head and looked just as surprised as he was.

'Who the fuck are you?' Kieran Clancy asked.

'Hawoo. I'm Froggy. Spawoo friend. Are you a good guy or a bad guy?'

Kieran frowned at the question, and then answered it.

'I'm a good guy.'

'Here!' Froggy said and handed Kieran the gun. Kieran took it and pulled Froggy to a standing position.

'Where are they, Froggy?' he asked. Froggy pointed in the direction of the bandstand.

Kieran ran towards the bandstand. Halfway there he could make out the two figures standing, now about three yards apart. They seemed to be just looking at each other. He slowed first and then stopped. Froggy arrived and stood beside him. On the bandstand Sparrow and Teddy remained standing apart.

'Well, well, Teddy, no gun? Oh dear. Are we a little bit scared now?' Sparrow goaded.

'Scared of you? Yeh little shit!' Teddy shouted. He lunged at Sparrow.

Sparrow sidestepped, and Teddy ran straight past him. Sparrow changed his stance to a boxing stance. Teddy smiled and threw off his overcoat.

'Okay, little champ. Let's see what yer made of.' Teddy took up a boxing stance too.

The two men prowled in a circle on the bandstand. Teddy feigned a blow at Sparrow who immediately threw up his guard. Teddy laughed. Sparrow moved forward towards Teddy. After two jabs and a punch to the stomach, Teddy reeled back. But he regained his footing and wiped his mouth. There was blood on his hand. He looked down at it.

'You're good!' Teddy said.

Sparrow motioned to Teddy to come forward and smiled at the man.

'Yeh, I am, and the bad news is, Teddy, I get fuckin' better.'

The two men closed on each other again. Sparrow got a jab off to the jaw, but his reach was not long enough. Teddy caught him with a punch to the ribs. It hurt. Teddy lunged again, this time using his sheer weight to get in a couple of jabs at Sparrow. One of them hit Sparrow across the bridge of the nose and blood began to pump from his nostrils.

Realising he couldn't out-reach Teddy, Sparrow sprang back from Teddy's lunging body. Teddy turned to face him again, more confident now. He began to move forward. Sparrow came in quickly, with a jab to the face and two body punches before Teddy could even gather himself.

Not many people realise it, but most fist fights or street fights last only thirty seconds. The amount of energy that's required to fight a street fight is usually used up within that time. Teddy was a street fighter. Sparrow was not. As Teddy began to wilt, Sparrow moved in to finish him off. A left to the ribs winded Teddy, and a right-cross opened a cut beneath his left eye. Teddy reeled back against the bandstand rails.

Now furious again, Teddy lunged. Sparrow sidestepped him and Teddy went straight past again. Teddy was reeling across the bandstand, Sparrow following him staying perfectly balanced. Teddy turned to make another lunge, but took a three-punch combination from Sparrow. He was dazed, disorientated and hurting.

Sparrow went in low now and came straight up Teddy's body with an uppercut. He heard the crunch of Teddy's jaw breaking, and one of Teddy's teeth flew out of his mouth. Dazed, Teddy reeled back against the rails. Sparrow went after him, but Teddy was now beginning to slide to the ground. Sparrow hauled Teddy up with his left hand and drew back his right. He heard the crowd begin to shout: 'Men-en-dez, Men-en-dez.' He heard Tommy Molloy, his coach, slapping the canvas and screaming, 'Throw the punch, throw the punch!'

Sparrow began to loosen his grip on Teddy. Over Teddy's shoulder he could see Froggy and Kieran Clancy standing together. He looked into Clancy's face. Kieran smiled and nodded once. Sparrow tightened his grip on Teddy's shirt, pulled him up and drove home a fifteen-year-old punch. Sparrow's fist made contact on the left-hand side of Teddy's face, just between his nose and his mouth. Sparrow let go his grip on Teddy's shirt. Teddy's head spun, blood spurted out of his mouth and his body tumbled over the edge of the bandstand onto the snow-covered grass.

Kieran Clancy smiled. He slipped his gun back into its holster. He put Teddy's gun into his pocket and slowly began to clap. Froggy imitated him. Sparrow, now crying, started to dance around the ring like a champ, with his hands raised in the air. Froggy joined him and danced with him in an identical pose.

Fifteen years had passed, but at last Sparrow had thrown that punch.

* * *

The McCabe home, 11.30pm

Mickey was sitting on the fireside chair in his pyjama bottoms and an Aston Villa tee shirt. Although the television was on and the revelry had begun in the run-up to midnight on RTE One, Mickey paid no attention. Instead, he stared into the flickering flames. Eileen entered the room with two cups of hot milk. As she came in Mickey looked up and smiled. Eileen squeezed her way into the armchair beside him and handed him his cup. Together they sat in the fireside chair sipping their hot milk.

✱ ✱ ✱

St Stephen's Green, Shelbourne Hotel entrance, 11.45pm

Sparrow didn't think there were this many police cars in Ireland, never mind around Stephen's Green. It seemed that everywhere he looked there were flashing blue lights and white police cars. Teddy was put into a police car, with his hands tied behind his back. Bubbles was taken away in a police ambulance. A uniformed guard was handcuffed to Simple Simon Williams. They sat in the back of the ambulance. Just before the ambulance doors were closed, Sparrow met Simon's gaze. It was cold and filled with hatred. Sparrow smiled at Simon Williams and gave him a little 'bye, bye' wave. The doors were slammed shut.

'Well, that's that, Sparrow. Lock, stock and barrel!' Kieran Clancy slapped Sparrow on the back.

'Yeh!' is all Sparrow answered. Sparrow was dishevelled, his shirt torn, his arms, chest and face ripped. He was bruised and battered from the fight. He was in a mess, but he felt elated. Kieran and Sparrow were joined now by Michael Malone. Michael introduced himself to Sparrow and extended his hand.

'Hello, Sparrow, I'm Michael Malone. I'm a fan. Jesus Christ, I don't know where Menendez is tonight, but wherever he is, he felt that punch!' As he said this, Michael let go with a big hefty West of Ireland laugh.

At first just a smile crossed Sparrow's face, but then he too joined in the laughter, as did Kieran Clancy. When the laughter died down, Kieran put his arm around Michael Malone's shoulders.

'Well, Michael, this is the best way I can think of to start the New Year!'

'New Year? New Year! Jesus! What time is it, Clancy?'

'Quarter to midnight, why?'

'Sam The Black!' Sparrow said.

'Who the black, what?' Kieran was totally confused.

'Sam The Black. Ah, it doesn't matter.' Sparrow waved a hand at Kieran and began to look furtively beyond the police cars.

'What are you looking for?' asked Kieran.

'A taxi. I have to get home! Now!' Sparrow's mind seemed to be somewhere else altogether.

'Sure, I'll drive you home – come on!' Kieran began to pull Sparrow towards the police car. With sirens blaring and lights flashing, they sped through Dublin city. As they reached the edge of Snuggstown at the Fairy Well, Sparrow said aloud, 'Happy New Year, fairies!'

Kieran gave him a sideways glance but made no comment. Suddenly, just as they came to Snuggstown village, Sparrow screamed, 'Stop the car!'

Kieran screeched to a halt. 'What? What's up!'

But his question was lost as Sparrow leaped from the car. Kieran jumped out too, looking confused. He became even more confused as Sparrow kicked at the large corrugated tin gate of a coalyard. Kieran looked around to make sure there were no police in sight, and made his way to Sparrow.

'Sparrow, Jesus Christ, what the fuck are you doing?' The question arrived simultaneously with the bursting of the gate. Without reply, Sparrow disappeared through the gateway. By the time Kieran reached the gate Sparrow was coming out again.

'It's okay, I've got it!' Sparrow said as he sprinted past Kieran back to the car.

'What the fuck ...' Still confused, Kieran sprinted back to the driver's side of the car. As he slammed the door, Sparrow prodded him on the shoulder.

'Move, Kieran, move!' Sparrow said, sounding as excited as a little kid.

* * *

The McCabe home, 12.00 midnight

Eileen and Mickey were sitting side-by-side on the fireside armchair. Eileen had her arm around Mickey and he was dozing lightly. On the television screen the revellers had nearly gone berserk. Thousands of people were gathered around Christ Church cathedral, awaiting the striking of the midnight bells. Eileen took the mug from Mickey's hand and placed it on the fireplace. She sat back and Mickey snuggled up to her, the light of the fire flickering across their faces. Mickey began to suck his thumb just as the Christ Church bells began to ring out midnight. The crowds cheered and the party was in full swing.

Suddenly there was a loud banging at the front door. Both Mickey and Eileen sat up with a start. Mickey looked at his mother.

'Sam The Black?' Mickey asked excitedly.

Slowly Eileen got up. She made her way to the front door with Mickey just a few paces behind her. A little frightened, Eileen slowly opened the door. Standing on her doorstep was Sparrow McCabe. He was dirty, dishevelled, wet and covered in blood.

Eileen and Sparrow stared at each other for a moment. It then dawned on Eileen that the man standing before her was not the Sparrow McCabe who had left her home fifteen days before, but the Sparrow McCabe who had left her life fifteen years before.

Sparrow had tears in his eyes. He tried to hold them back but he couldn't, and they streaked down his face as if he was wearing mascara. Slowly he brought his hand up to chest level. It was closed in a fist. He opened it. In the palm of his hand was a lump of black coal.

'Happy New Year, Eileen,' Sparrow said.

And Eileen knew it would be.

OTHER BOOKS BY BRENDAN O'CARROLL

published by
The O'Brien Press

THE BEST-SELLING, HILARIOUS MRS BROWNE TRILOGY

THE MAMMY

Agnes Browne is a strong woman – strong enough to cope with widowhood, seven children, a tenement flat in The Jarro in the heart of Dublin city, and the daily grind of her Moore Street stall. But even strong women need a little help and a dream of their own to keep them going ...

THE CHISELLERS

Three years after her husband Redser's death, Agnes Browne soldiers on, being mother, father and referee to her family of seven. Helped out financially by her eldest, and hormonally by the amorous Pierre, Agnes copes with tragedy, success – and relocation to the 'wilds of the country' in suburban Finglas. And when an unscrupulous gangster threatens the family's dreams he learns a costly lesson: when you take on one of Mrs Browne's children you take on them all!

THE GRANNY

Agnes, now forty-seven, a granny and happily widowed for thirteen years, watches over the changing fortunes of her family – marriage, prison, broken relationships, literary success. Then the family begins to fragment and it seems that not even their mammy's iron will can bring them together again. But you can never write off Agnes Browne!